BODY
SNATCHERS

BY

Rozè

Cover design by Todd Chapman
Cover Photograph(s): iStock
Interior Design by Nancey Flowers
Edited by Chandra Sparks Taylor–www.chandrasparkstaylor.com

First Flowers in Bloom trade paperback printing 2011

For more information, or to contact the author, send correspondence to:
Flowers in Bloom Publishing, LLC.
2152 Ralph Avenue
#421
Brooklyn, NY 11234
www.flowersinbloompublishing.com

Library of Congress Cataloging-in-Publication Data
Body Snatchers/ Jermine Benton - 1st ed.
Library of Congress Control Number: 2011931915
1. African Americans–Fiction. 2. Criminals–Family relationships–Fiction. 3.
Street life– Fiction. 4. Urban fiction. 5. Haiti–Fiction. 6. Gangs–Fiction.
7. Triangles (Interpersonal relations)– Fiction

ISBN: 978-0-9798614-3-7
ISBN: 0-9798614-3-8

10 9 8 7 6 5 4 3 2 1
First Paperback Edition

Printed in the United States

Acknowledgments

First and foremost, I want to dedicate this book to all the Haitian people who died in the earthquake on January 10, 2010. My condolences and love goes out to everyone who lost a loved one. My Haitian people are strong and resilient, and I know that eventually we will overcome the turmoil we are currently experiencing. Haiti was the first country to free itself from the grips of slavery, and I know this is only another obstacle put in front of us over which we will triumph. Hopefully change will come soon for Haiti. This novel is a written testimony of my trust and love for my family and country.

I also want to dedicate my achievements to two special women in my life. It is because of them that I strive to become a better person. Negative intentions and judgment are not part of their character, and forever I will love you more. First, is my mother, Claudette, and second is my sister Jadey. Ma and Jay, I love you both. This book would not be possible if not for the love, dedication, and support I received from my family. I'd like to send a shout-out to my big brother Patrick, cousin Roselyn, and eldest sister Olivia. Also to my extended family, Billy Steele, Dimo, Ricky, LB, A, Nitty, M-dot, Black Lion, Rolex, Ras, Wes, Quiet Storm, David House, Afrika, Skully, Shower, Mad Indian, Smiley, Dappa, Jabba, Heathcliffe, Boodabye, and Jubba. If I missed anyone, I promise to hold down on the next run.

1

Jerry

December 2, 1999

My mother's life was spared.

A few months ago, my mother was closing her restaurant for the night when two Zenglendo, gang bangers, entered the place, demanding money. The restaurant was popular in the community and sold black rice and peas, d'ri djon djon, fried pork shoulders, also known as griot, chicken, and some of the best Haitian patties in town. Unfortunately, unemployment was at an all-time high and her business wasn't faring as well as it used to. When she told the hoodlums she didn't have any money, they set her restaurant on fire. The damage and devastation caused by the arson forced my mother out of business, and she was unable to rebuild. In order to make ends meet, she was forced into taking odd jobs in the neighborhood, serving as a housekeeper and babysitter.

We lived a little more than an hour away from the city in a small town called Jacmel. Our house rested on a hilltop. It was similar to a one-bedroom apartment, but without the amenities. It consisted of a bedroom where my mom, pop, and baby sister slept; a kitchen; and a living room where me and my two brothers slept on the couch and floor. Our bathroom was separate from the house, and since we didn't have indoor plumbing, we had to fill plastic barrels every day with water drawn from the well for bathing. We also had to purchase water for drinking. That's the customary way of life for most Haitians. The toilet was a large hole dug in the ground, surrounded by cement blocks housed within a shack. My father instructed me how build it from scratch, and it was made out of sand and straw.

There are only five of us left now, since my father suddenly died seven years ago from a heart attack. My brother Johnny was twenty years old when my pop died and is ten years older than me and my twin brother, David. My younger sister, Loria, was only five years old and now faced life without a father.

About two months ago, my mother told David and me that our aunt, who was living in New York, was willing to take us both in. We desperately want to go, but didn't have enough money to obtain our Visas. The other day, my mom found out through a family friend that a guy could get us to the States by boat. Still, we didn't have enough money to pay our fare for that either. David and I dropped out of school and resorted to robbing everyone wherever we could.

One particular night, we had our eyes set on two local crooked cops who frequented our neighborhood. You could barely see their car parked down a dark alley because the only light came from a street lamp at the far end of the corner. I was wearing a black dingy sweater, blue jeans, and sneakers as was David who was crouched down beside me. David and I are identical twins. We have gray eyes and a caramel complexion. We inherited our good looks from our mother and our height and wavy hair from our father. Only our immediate family members are able to tell us apart.

I could only see one head in the back of the squad car. I looked over at David, and he shrugged to say he couldn't find his partner either.

"What the fuck?" I said, wondering where the other cop was.

We were speaking in English now since we learned it in school. However, we only spoke English around certain people or when we didn't want others to understand us. Otherwise, we spoke Creole.

"Go ahead. I got your back," he said.

David saw movement on the right side of the alley. He noticed the second cop walking out of a small shack holding a bag in his hand. The cop said something inaudible and began walking toward the car. David followed with a metal pipe held tightly in his hand.

I picked up a pipe near my foot and crept slowly around to the other side of the car. I was about five steps away from the passenger's side when suddenly I heard a crushing sound. I turned to see David bashing the cop's head in with the pipe. I ducked behind the car when I heard the door fly open. As the sound of the second cop's footsteps quickly moved toward me, I could see his shadow grow bigger. I popped up and smashed my pipe against his mug, and the cop dropped in agony, grabbing his face.

"Ah, you dead!" the cop screamed.

As he fumbled to reach for his gun, I jumped on him and started beating him to near death.

"Hurry up! We gotta go!" David shouted.

He grabbed the brown bag from off the ground and kicked the cop in his groin and began running toward me.

I reached inside the other police officer's pocket and grabbed his money along with his revolver.

"Alright, come on," I said, feeling satisfied.

We ran off into the night and never looked back.

2

David

I considered my brother Jerry and me different from each other. Being the oldest (six minutes), he had it kind of hard growing up. My father always seemed to have it out for him, and I never understood why. Whenever my father arrived home, the first thing he would do when he walked through the door would be to make a beeline toward Jerry. He'd come home drunk sometimes, then would order Jerry to do all the odd chores. If he didn't like how Jerry did them, he'd beat him. My mother never spoke up to defend him or even tried to intervene, causing Jerry to feel a little animosity and resentment toward her. When we went out on our shopping sprees, Jerry would let out his frustration on people and sometimes take things to the extreme. Don't get it twisted, 'cause I can get wild too, but I'm considered the reserved and humble brother. I usually like to think and weigh my options first before making a move. Times are always hard in Haiti, so there isn't much to think about, except scheming about ways to get money.

Tonight, I'm going out with my girlfriend, Fifi. We've been kicking it for about a year now. We met at Begal Beach, just outside of Port-au-Prince. She was at the beach with her best friend Sophie and her cousin Mario. Jerry noticed her cousin first, because he was wearing a Cuban link gold bracelet and chain set. And Jerry, being Jerry, was thinking of a way to stick him.

Jerry didn't have to say anything to me since I already knew what he was thinking. Before he could utter a word, I looked at him and told him to leave this one alone. He tried to act like he didn't know what I was referring to, but after a second glance, he knew I was serious about this one. Jerry's response was, "You need to get your head out of the clouds and focus on getting money. You're such a sucker for love, man."

I just ignored him and continued focusing all my attention on Fifi. After a couple of minutes of trying to figure out my approach, I decided to wait until she was alone. As soon as I saw her cousin and her best friend go into the water, I instinctively made my move. As I walked in her direction, I noticed her rubbing suntan lotion on her legs and knew this was the perfect opportunity.

"Do you need help putting that on your back, sweetheart?" I asked.

She looked up, shading her eyes from the sun as she gave me a quick once-over and I smiled. From that moment on I knew she was mine.

We spent the rest of the day together at the beach, getting to know each other. Her best friend was trying to get me to hook her up with Jerry, but he wasn't interested in her and he was missing in action for the remainder of the day.

We continued spending more time together, mostly at her house, because she lived in a mini mansion, and it was more comfortable. It was her uncle Chico's home. Her cousin Mario also lived there, but he was away at school for most of the year. At first, I would visit when I knew her uncle was at work, but as we got closer, I was there almost every other night. Her uncle Chico was into politics and ran a drug spot. Fifi held a lot of resentment toward him because of something that happened between her father and him. She blamed Uncle Chico for her father's death. I didn't care for him either because he was extremely arrogant.

Jerry wasn't too happy about the amount of time Fifi and I were spending together. Whenever Jerry and Fifi were around each other, within fifteen minutes, an argument would erupt. Jerry felt she was taking up too much of my personal time and that I should be out getting money with him. Fifi just didn't understand why he always had such an attitude, but this was the first time either of us had ever had a long-term relationship, and Jerry and I were usually inseparable.

Fifi lived a sheltered life and was not exposed to the hardness of the streets. Her uncle Chico was very strict and enrolled her in a school for girls. He wouldn't let her go anywhere unless her cousin Mario was with her. He finally loosened up a little when she was in her last year of school, but that was only because he was preoccupied with his own personal business. Fifi wasn't like the average girl I messed with. She was intelligent, classy, and sexy, and although she wasn't street savvy, she could still hold her own. Whenever Jerry would say some of his smart remarks to her, she would give him one right back. I would just sit back and laugh at them going back and forth.

I planned on meeting Fifi at Cite Soleil restaurant for dinner and wanted to pick her brain about a plan I was devising in order to get money. When I arrived at the restaurant, Fifi was already there waiting for me. She was sitting at the table near the balcony, wearing her red strapless dress, and she looked so sexy with her hair pulled back. Her brown skin skin glistened in the moonlight.

"Hi, sweetie," Fifi said, looking more gorgeous than ever.

"Hi, sexy," I responded, sitting down across from her.

I waved to the waiter and ordered my usual glass of Barbancourt, and Fifi ordered a glass of sweet red liquor called Ti'rose. Once our drinks arrived, Fifi sat back and took a sip of her drink. She patiently waited for me to start the conversation

I started off with small talk, asking her how her day was.

"My day was good, but kind of busy. I went out with Sophie, and we went shopping. Afterward, we ran a few errands around town," Fifi said, taking another sip of her drink.

"I know you bought something, so what did you get?" I asked, leaning back in my seat.

Fifi smiled then said, "You know me so well. Yes, I did buy a handbag because I couldn't resist." She put her hand on the red-and-black purse that was on the table.

I looked down and chuckled, then took a drink from my glass.

Fifi placed her left hand on top of mine. "I want you to spend the weekend with me at my house. My uncle is out of town. He went to the Dominican Republic, so you don't have to worry about leaving in the middle of the night."

"Word? When did he leave?" I asked, straightening up in my seat. She managed to pique my attention.

"He left the other day on business," she said, rolling her eyes.

"Alright, no problem. I'm there," I said, rubbing her hand.

"Stop being naughty, David," Fifi said and laughed.

The waiter came back to our table and took our order. As we waited for our food, Fifi walked off to the bathroom. I sat back in my chair and thought, *I didn't even have to ask her anything because she basically told me everything I wanted to know. Tonight is going better than I expected.*

When I got home from my date with Fifi I found Jerry and my mother sitting in the yard talking. I approached my mother and gave her a kiss on the cheek and nodded at Jerry.

"David, I was just telling your brother I got a message from the guy who is supposed to take y'all to the States," my mother said.

"What did he say?" I asked.

"The boat is leaving day after tomorrow. They said between 2:00 to 3:00 A.M., so, you two better start packing because they won't wait for you," she said as she stood and walked into the house.

I took a seat next Jerry on top of a crate and said, "I may have a way for us to get some serious money before going to the States."

"Really! And what is that?" Jerry asked, looking at me.

"The other day when I was at Chico's house, I accidentally walked into a room and saw him putting money into a safe in his office. He had his back toward the door, so he didn't see me. I quickly moved into the corner and watched him punch in the code and lock the safe. I know there's thousands of dollars in there, so you can figure out what I have in mind."

Jerry smiled and said, "Oh yes, I can. It's about time to collect."

"We should hit up his place tomorrow night before we leave for our trip. Fifi told me tonight that Chico is in the Dominican Republic on business, so we don't have to worry about that fool," I said.

"Dominican Republic, that's perfect. Is she down with the heist?"

"No. She knows nothing about this. And since I know the combination and the location of the money, you're going to have to pretend you're me and distract her while I sneak in and take the dough," I said, rubbing my chin. "It would be easier than me trying to map out the house for you. More than likely you'll end up getting lost and tear the place up in frustration."

"Oh brother, you already know we don't get along, but I'll do whatever we have to in order to get this money," Jerry said, shaking his head in disgust.

"Yeah, we need this dough. Tomorrow is the day, and we're gonna make this happen."

3

Jerry

December 23, 1999

"Tomorrow can't come soon enough," David said aloud while waiting in the living room as I got ready. I could tell he was anxious to go to Chico's house. While waiting, he sipped on some Barbancourt to ease his nerves.

"You ready?" I asked, tucking my gun under my shirt and grabbing the rest of the liquor.

"Yeah, come on," David said, following me into the kitchen.

"Y'all not eating before y'all go out?" Moms asked with love in her voice and concern in her eyes.

"No, we're not hungry," I replied. "We'll be home early anyway."

We followed her outside to where she was cooking. We didn't have a traditional stove, so she cooked over a charcoal burner that was located in the yard.

"You two better be back early. Don't forget you have to pack," she warned, pointing a finger in our direction.

"We won't," I promised, kissing her cheek.

"Bye, Ma," Jerry said, doing the same.

We took off down the hill. By the time we got to Chico's house, we had finished the entire bottle of liquor. We were feeling nice and full of adrenaline. This job should be a piece of cake," I said and my brother agreed.

"Alright, listen, you go and keep Fifi busy while I sneak in behind you. Since I know where the money is, I won't be long. Once I have the money I will signal you by ringing the bell saying I'm here to pick you up." David said, with a serious tone in his voice.

David knew I couldn't stand Fifi and that we didn't get along. We were always arguing because she's loose at the mouth. But tonight, I have to look at the bigger picture.

"Yeah, yeah, I'm gonna leave the door unlocked once I get inside," I said, walking up to Chico's front gate.

I had only been there a couple of times to pick up David and had waited outside. If Chico was outside, he would usually give me some weed. He always had something slick to say, whenever he saw me.

"Here, go and smoke with your little friends. I know you guys aren't used to the quality shit I got," he would tease in a very condescending tone.

I rang the bell on the gate and waited for Fifi to come. Moments later, she opened the gateway and jumped on me.

"Hey, baby," she said, giving me a very long, sensuous kiss.

"Hey," I responded nearly losing my balance from the kiss and the alcohol.

"I'm not staying long tonight. I have something to do with my brother later," I quickly explained.

"Oh, not Jerry again! Whatever," Fifi said with an attitude.

I wanted to respond with something slick, but I held my tongue and followed her inside.

Fifi was petite with a milk chocolate complexion, shoulder-length hair, and dark, mysterious eyes. She always hid her figure by wearing baggy clothes, but tonight she wore a knee-length silk robe that left little to my imagination. I walked behind her and glanced over my shoulder, only to find David grilling me. I smiled at him and continued to follow her into the house. I shut the door and left it unlocked.

This dude's house was plush. He had impressive portraits neatly arranged on pure white walls and expensive crystal chandeliers hanging from the ceiling. The black-and-white marble floor tiles matched the furniture perfectly. When I walked past the living room, I noticed a large floor-model TV with an elaborate sound system. There were speakers in each corner of the room. *I can definitely see why David loved being here,* I thought.

"What the fuck?" I said under my breath. All of a sudden, I saw Fifi's cousin Mario coming toward me.

"What's up, David?" he asked as he walked past me.

"Come on, silly!" Fifi giggled, and pulled me into her room.

"What's he doing here?" I asked as I shut the door closed to her room.

"He won't be here long," she said and began removing her robe.

I was about to say something, but I instantly forgot once I saw Fifi undressing. Boy, I was wrong because this chick had a crazy body. Her titties were full and plump, about the size of juicy cantaloupes, and her nipples were hard. I looked at her thick legs and worked my eyes up to her pleasure zone, and I noticed her perfectly shaped triangle.

"Wh-what you doing?" I stammered, caught off guard.

"I've been thinking, and it's time," she replied shyly.

"It's time? Time for what?"

"Yeah, I'm ready," she said in a seductive voice and walked toward me.

I don't think I should have drank so much on a empty stomach, I thought as I stared at Fifi's naked body. It was hard to believe David still hadn't fucked her for all of his boasting. Before I could protest, she wrapped her arms around my shoulders and started kissing me. Her sweet aroma and soft, juicy lips had me open. I started touching and sucking all parts of her body that I had no business touching. Before I knew it, my belt was unbuckled and my pants were down, and the next thing I knew I was deep inside of her. "Damn this is good" I said as I thrust myself into her and she screamed for mercy.

Her nails found the center of my back as she gripped me with pleasure. I looked down and noticed that there were spots of blood on my shorts and the sheets. I knew I should stop, but she was feeling so good. Fifi's pussy was tight, wet and warm. She was feeling so good that within fifteen minutes I couldn't hold back anymore, and I released. However, I never missed a beat and continued stroking and was hard again within seconds. My thoughts were elsewhere until Fifi's grip loosened and she lay still.

Suddenly she jumped up and yelled, "Stop! Did you hear that?"

Knowing if I didn't do what I was about to, she would blow everything up. I two pieced her, knocking her out. To ensure she stayed unconscious, I picked up an object from the nightstand and clocked her for good measure. I then grabbed my shorts and gun and ran out. I followed the noise and stumbled upon David tussling with Mario in what I suspected was Chico's room. I ran over to him and gun butted Mario in the head. He fell to the ground in pain, holding his head in his hands.

"You got the money?" I asked.

"Not yet," he replied while getting up from the floor.

Seeing David's face, bloody and scratched from fighting with Mario, got me tight. I felt a surge of rage shoot through me. My fingers didn't hesitate to remove the safety latch and pull the trigger. The force behind the shots caused Mario's body to hit the floor immediately. His body convulsed and within seconds it was over. He never saw what was coming.

David jumped back, stunned from my actions and the loud shots.

"What the fuck did you do that for?" he shouted.

I looked down at Mario's bullet-ridden corpse without remorse, shrugged, and walked away.

David walked over to the safe and said, "We fucked up now and killed Mario. We definitely have to get out of Haiti now." He quickly emptied the contents of the safe into the duffle bags and we bounced.

4

Jerry

December 24, 1999

"Oh my God, David!" my mother screamed when we entered the house and she saw David's face.

"Some bullies tried to rob me," David lied.

"Jerry, what happened?" she pleaded, almost in tears.

"They thought he had money," I said, walking past her.

I walked straight into her bedroom and placed a bag of money beneath her bed. I knew my mother would find the bag eventually because she was always cleaning. The house was dark because of a power outage. In Haiti, we didn't have a consistent power supply, so almost every night half the country lost power, unless you could afford a generator as a backup source.

My mother always kept candles around for times like this.

I jumped when I heard a voice behind me.

"I thought you were going to play with me today," my little sister Loria said from the doorway.

"Come here," I said. She walked over and I set her down on my lap. "You know David and I are leaving?"

"Where are you going?" Loria asked.

"To America."

"Where is America?" she asked curiosly.

"It's a place where we can live a good life. Live big dreams."

"Don't you like it here with me?"

"It's not you, Lory."

"Then, why are you leaving?" she asked as tears formed in her eyes.

Loria is petite and appeared younger than kids her age. She was a miniature replica of our mother. She has long, silky hair that Mom kept in pigtails. She is chocolate brown and has huge puppy-dog eyes that made me melt every time I looked into them. After Dad died, she became quiet and kind of distant. She had been a daddy's girl, but after our fathers death she came to talk and play with me occasionally. She was a bit of a loner and didn't even like playing with the other kids in the neighborhood.

"I wanna come with you," she whined.

I thought about it for a second and figured I would send for her when things were right.

"You can't, but I promise I'll come back for you and mommy, okay?"

"You promise?"

"I promise. Now give me a hug," I said, wrapping my arms around her small frame.

"Now, let me go say good-bye to Mommy," I said, wiping the tears from her eyes.

I tickled her until she started to cry tears of laughter, then I walked into the kitchen to find my mother still babying David. I hated when she treated him like a little kid.

"We have to leave now, before it gets too late," I said to David.

"Do you need anything?" Mom asked us.

"No, Ma," we replied in unison.

"You two better not give Kathy a hard time in America," she said seriously.

"We won't," David said.

"Now, give me a hug."

We both gave her a hug and a kiss, just as Johnny walked into the house.

"You're leaving tonight, huh?" he asked, looking at us.

"Yeah, man," I said, moving toward him.

Johnny could have passed for a triplet if it wasn't for his height and the fact that he looked older than us. We rarely spoke or hung out together since we lived different lives. He thought he was some kind of pimped-out Casanova or Don Juan. Still, our hearts remained loyal to one another.

"I'm looking forward to seeing you out there someday," I said, referring to America.

"Nah, Haiti is where I belong, kiddo. I love her too much to abandon her," Johnny said, grinning.

I chuckled, then picked up the bag.

"You crazy," I said, smiling.

"You two just take it easy in America," Johnny warned, giving us a knowing look.

I chuckled and gave him a pound. David did the same.

"Bye, everyone!" we shouted, running out the door.

As Johnny watched us run down the hill, he laughed and shouted, "I love you guys."

5

David

e ran down the hill to the street, carrying our bags and trying to find a van that was going to Cap Haitian, where the boat was supposed to leave. The buses in Haiti were like cargo buses. They transported produce livestock and on occasion, passengers. There were usually bags of charcoal or lumber stored in the bottom of the truck, and passengers had to climb to the top of the load just to find a place to sit. The truck never came to a complete stop and would only slow down just enough for you to jump off. After what seemed like hours of walking, we spotted a small van heading in our direction, but it was crowded. We ran along the side of the van and jumped on, continuing to our destination. Half the people on the van were going to Cap Haitian for the same reasons we were.

When we finally arrived, there were several people waiting in front of the pickup spot. As we all stood waiting for the boat to arrive, Jerry and I decided to talk to some of them who were hanging around. One guy was heading to Canada to live with his brother. He told us his cousin made the trip about a year ago, and he was now living and working the good life there. Another couple was heading to Florida. The wife was pregnant, and they wanted their child to be born an American citizen. They were planning to stay at the husband's family house until they got on their feet. Everyone had a different destination, but with the same focus in mind: to get out of Haiti and make some money. The boat finally arrived, and I looked at Jerry and said, "How the hell are all these people supposed to fit on this boat?"

"I don't know. I just know we're on this bitch," Jerry said, running toward the boat.

The past two days had been the worst. I woke up hearing Jerry arguing with a man whom he said was trying to pick his pockets. The boat's maximum capacity was only for twenty people, but there was double that amount onboard. The entire ride was bumpy and noisy. If someone wasn't arguing or complaining, then they were trying to fight in the cramped space. As the boat reached closer to the shore of Oyster Cove, Florida, a bright light appeared out of nowhere. Someone on a nearby boat flashed us.

"Stop your boat, or we will shoot!" a loud voice boomed over a bullhorn.

All at once, men and women grabbed their kids and jumped into the water. In the same instant, shots started to rain. I grabbed the bag of money from Jerry and handed him my gun. Jerry started shooting with both guns, trying to cover me. Fortunately, we both knew how to swim well—when Pops was alive we did this regularly as a family.

I could hear the bullets whizzing past my ears and landing in the water. Women and men were screaming, either from fear of being hit or from losing a loved one. I heard two shots ring out and saw a coast guard fall overboard. Someone took his gun and started to shoot back at the coast guard's ship.

Machine guns were being fired around us.

Once I reached the shore, I waited for Jerry to catch up and grabbed his hand to help him out of the water. We looked around and saw a highway beyond the trees. While we ran toward the trees, we saw a woman crying and pleading to a coast guard for her daughter's life.

Jerry shot the guard and he instantly let her go. The woman got up, thanked us, then ran back to the water. I took the guard's gun out of his holster and searched his pockets.

"Let's go!" Jerry shouted and ran toward the highway.

We ran along the side of the highway, trying to signal a car to stop. I looked over at Jerry, then realized why the cars weren't stopping. No one was going to stop for two wet and disheveled black guys on the highway. I searched for the slowest moving vehicle and jumped in front of a van, aiming my pistol at the driver. The man behind the wheel skidded to a halt, and threw his hands up in the air. Jerry ran to the car and opened the back door. I jumped in the front seat and told the man to drive.

"Wh-where to?" he stuttered with an accent.

"Miami."

6

Chico's House - Haiti

December 25, 1999

In Haiti, Chico was the man to see if you wanted or needed anything. There was nothing going on that he didn't know about. Chico supported men into getting into the ambassador's seat and even presidential ones. In return, they turned the other cheek to his illegal affairs. Chico started at the bottom of the totem pole, just like everyone else. Growing up, Fifi's father, Sunny, along with Chico, began robbing, killing, and kidnapping to get money and power. They watched their parents turn into worthless drug addicts. Through their neglect, they found their love out on the streets and formed one of the most infamous posses ever known, the Zenglendo. This organization gave them a sense of belonging, love, and power. Before long this became a way of life for them.

One day, while Chico was out with one of his girlfriends, Sunny got wind that some drug dealers were trying to get rid of some products at wholesale. Trying to impress Chico, he went out searching for these guys and ended up getting shot in the back by one of the dudes. Chico now became the guardian of Fifi, who was only three years old at the time. Chico later made contact with a guy in the Dominican Republic named Carlo. He fell in love with his sister-in-law, Maria, who conceived their first and only son, Mario. There was no one in this world he loved more than Mario. Chico showered him with the luxuries that other kids in their country weren't fortunate enough to have. He was grooming him to become the heir of his throne to take over the family business.

However, now all of Chico's dreams were shattered. He couldn't believe this could happen to him as he cried over his son's dead body.

"Oh, Mario, my beautiful son!" he cried.

Fifi regained consciousness hours after Jerry attacked her. She felt like her skull had been cracked with a crowbar. Fifi touched her face and felt a massive bruise and her nose felt dislodged. It was probably broken.

She remained in the darkness of her room crying after realizing David had become someone she didn't know by attacking her and leaving her like a dead animal on the side of the road. A day later she emerged like a frightened cat, not knowing who or what awaited her beyond her bedroom door. Once again she found herself crouched in the corner of Mario's room, crying and hugging herself after she discovered the body on the floor. She was confused and didn't know how Mario wound up dead.

What the hell is going on? David had never even raised his voice to me in the past, so why would he hit me, kill Mario, and steal from us? What was this all about? This was not like the David I know and love. It just doesn't make sense, Fifi thought.

Chico turned around and looked at her with venomous eyes, then grabbed her. "Who did this?" he yelled, shaking Fifi, looking for answers.

She looked terrified as she cried out, "I swear, I don't know, Uncle Chico!"

One of Chico's guards rushed into the room, holding a videotape.

Out of breath, the stocky guard gasped, "I think this will tell us what we need to know!"

Chico threw Fifi to the side like a rag doll and grabbed the video from the guard. Quickly, he walked directly to his entertainment unit and inserted the video. He stood pacing as he closely examined it, looking for clues. He fast forwarded the tape to later in the evening and saw Fifi walking her boyfriend into the house. Two minutes later, he noticed someone else walking into his house unannounced.

"Isn't that your boyfriend's brother? Why is he walking in two minutes after y'all? Who let him in, and why does he keep looking back, like someone is following him?" Chico asked Fifi.

Fifi was standing behind him and saw Jerry walk in, after she and David had entered the house.

"I don't know," Fifi responded, totally confused.

The tape suddenly stopped and was replaced by black-and-white static.

"What the fuck is going on? Là Merdë!" Chico shouted angrily.

Although the tape had ended, the image of one of the twins sneaking into his house was more than enough evidence for him.

"Jerry and David are behind this, and I know it! All fingers point to the twins! My only son is dead, and my money is missing!" Chico yelled, looking at Fifi with vengeance in his eyes.

"I'm going to find them and kill them!"

7

Twin's House - Haiti

The following evening, Johnny, the twin's older brother, was home preparing for his date. His mother was in her room with her daughter Loria, combing her hair and getting ready for their yearly trip to Grandma's house.

"Mommy, how long is it going to take us to get to Grandma's house?" Loria asked with excitement in her voice.

"Loria, you ask me this question every year, and I tell you the same thing. It's going to take three hours to get there because Grandma lives on the other side of the mountains," her mother said, while parting her hair.

"I wish Jerry and David were coming with us," Loria said, turning around to look at her mother.

"I know, sweetie, but they're on their way to your auntie's house in America where they are going to find jobs and save money so that we can go to America too," she explained.

"I can't wait to go to America, Mommy," Loria said.

"Me too, sweetie. Me too," she responded.

Johnny walked into his mother's room and took the iron off the top of the dresser.

"Big plans tonight, Casanova?" his mother asked, smiling.

"You know it, Mom. I'm going to Le Lambi with this hottie I met in Carrefour about a month ago," Johnny said and smiled at her before walking out of the room.

As he ironed his shirt, he started thinking about his brothers leaving for the States. *Haiti is one of the poorest countries in the western hemisphere, but I still love it. We were the first country to fight and win our independence in 1803. The countries in higher power feel that because we're black, we're inferior to them, so they blackball us from the chance we deserve to become a sustainable country. We were abandoned and left to fend for ourselves. The media only shows the violence and poverty-stricken neighborhoods, but I see a culture of beautiful people. Every day is a recession over here, but we still manage to have fun and know how to survive. Our country is filled with beautiful women from various ethnicities: French, Hispanic, and of course, African.*

Tonight, I have a date with Dorothy, and I can't wait because she has an ass that would make a broke man steal just to trick on her. Those beautiful hazel-colored eyes, plump lips, and honey-kissed skin drive me crazy. My man jumps every time she blows a kiss my way. Tonight is the night I finally get a chance to be alone with her.

"She's gonna be mine," Johnny said out loud.

Johnny's thoughts were interrupted when he heard someone banging on the door.

"Johnny!" his mother shouted from her room.

"Yeah," he yelled back, resting the iron on the ground.

"Go get the door," she said.

"I got it," he replied.

When Johnny opened the door, he saw David's girlfriend Fifi, her uncle Chico, and three guys with guns. Before he could slam the door shut, Chico pushed his way inside. Johnny never got a chance to warn his mother.

8

Twins House - Haiti

Chico and his goons pushed their way into the house and were not leaving until they got some answers. They grabbed Johnny and pushed him onto the floor.

"Where are your brothers?" Chico demanded, spit flying from his mouth.

Johnny was on his knees, while Chico's men held his arms.

"I-I don't know," he said weakly.

After hearing strange voices, their mother told Loria to stay put and rushed out of the room to see what all the commotion was about. She walked out and found Johnny lying on the floor with a gun pointed to his back. Chico was standing in the middle of the house, along with three of his bodyguards while Fifi stood next to the door.

"What is going on here?" she asked, shocked to see what was happening.

"We're looking for Jerry and David! Where are they?" Chico demanded.

"We don't know! They don't live here anymore!" their mother responded desperately.

"Search the house!" Chico commanded one of his men.

Fifi watched all the action quietly from the corner. She felt bad for the family, but knew better than to try and intervene. She looked over at David's mother and watched as she kneeled in a praying position, pleading to Chico.

"Please, they do not live here anymore! Let my son go!" she cried.

"For the last time, where are they?" Chico growled.

One of the men pulled a bag out from under the bed and returned to the living room. He opened it and poured the contents on the floor, which was littered with Haitian and American money. Chico looked at her with burning anger.

"I swear, I don't know where that came from!" she said in amazement.

"So, then how did this bag of money get into your room, you lying bitch!" Chico spat.

One of Chico's goons pushed her down and pinned her to the floor, placing his muddy boots onto her back. The other guard kicked her in the midsection, and she cried out in pain.

Johnny broke loose from the goons and proceeded to rush the guy, but Chico grabbed him, threw him onto the floor and began hitting him with the butt of his gun. .

Fifi couldn't watch anymore, so she walked out the front door and wandered toward the back of the house.

Chico and his goons continued with their thrashing. They tortured Johnny until he became unconscious. He had a large gash in the back of his head, and blood was spewing from different parts of his body. His mother was beaten beyond recognition. Her eyes were swollen shut, and her jaw was cracked from being kicked by steel-toed boots.

"What's next?" one of the goons asked.

Chico didn't get a chance to answer the question because his telephone rang. It was an urgent call from one of his political associates.

Meanwhile, Fifi was still in the back of the house, sobbing and praying her uncle would stop. Suddenly, she heard a noise. She stopped crying and looked around to see where the noise was coming from. As she approached the opposite side of the house, she noticed a figure running behind a pile of charcoal.

Slowly she walked toward the pile to see what was stirring. She was a few feet shy from discovering what was hiding behind the house when suddenly, she heard her uncle's voice. She stopped dead in her tracks and rushed toward the front of the house before he came looking for her. She didn't want her uncle taking his rage out on her. As she slid in the backseat of the car, she thought, *I have to return later.*

As Chico walked out of the house to wrap up his call, he looked back and said to his gang, "You know what to do."

Moments later several rounds of gunfire filled the air, and as they drove off into the night, the backdrop of the burning house lit the sky.

9

Jerry

The ride to Miami was exhausting. All the drama and suspense left me tired. I found out the driver we stopped on the highway was also Haitian. He told us almost every week, there were boatloads of Haitians and Cubans being killed or getting caught trying to flee to the States. Some of the Cubans got to stay because they had immunity. Unfortunately for Haitians, we were not as lucky and got sent back. Some Haitians were so successful because they had been transporting people for so long that they chose to smuggle immigrants as an occupation. The driver took us to a place called Little Haiti. The women there were beautiful and came in all shapes and sizes; flavors from Jamaican, Indian, Latin, and American. You name it, they were there. Our fun was short lived, however. The truck we were supposed to be on was leaving for New York City that night.

The ride to New York took a day and a half. We were dropped off at Rockefeller Center in Manhattan. The weather was unbelievably cold, and we were not prepared since we were still wearing the clothes we left Haiti in. There were so many people outside wearing big coats, hats, and scarves, and there were a lot of colorful toys displayed. We couldn't buy any warm clothes because the money we had was still wet. All we had on us was what the driver gave us, which was a tight denim jacket, an I Love New York sweatshirt, and a trucker's hat.

I don't know how long we walked, but during the whole time, all the lights and big buildings had me awestruck. I overheard people saying,

"Happy New Year." I guess this was how they celebrated the New Year.

"Jerry, look!" David exclaimed, pointing upward.

When I looked up, I saw a big shiny ball and thousands of balloons falling from the sky. Everyone was jumping and giving each other hugs, so I shrugged and began jumping along with them. I grabbed the first girl I saw and hugged her and screamed, "Happy New Year!"

The cab ride to the house was very relaxing and scenic. We stopped at the address my mother had given us. There was a school located directly across the street, which I later learned was Junior High School 217. The house was painted beige and had a small black gate in the front. I heard music nearby and figured someone was having a party. Jerry and I walked up to the porch and banged on the door. The lights on the porch came on, and the door swung open. Aunt Kathy opened the door with a big smile. She was the spitting image of my mother— with the same long hair, brown eyes, and milk-chocolate skin.

"Oh my God, look how big y'all got!" she yelled, pulling us inside.

Aunt Kathy spoke English as though she was born in America, without an accent. When she turned eighteen, my grandfather paid an American man to marry her so she could become an American citizen. She wasted no time and immediately enrolled in school to obtain her degrees. Now, she is a registered nurse at Mary Immaculate Hospital, located off Hillside Avenue.

"Look at you two. Come on in! Let's get you a change of clothes," Aunt Kathy said.

With that we entered our new life in America.

10

David

The house was hooked up. The first floor was adorned with souvenirs and African artifacts. The living room walls were mocha and had gold and tan furniture throughout. The kitchen was immaculate. It had a high wooden table in the center of the room with a stainless-steel refrigerator and state-of-the-art appliances. Next, Aunt Kathy lead us to the basement, which was where our room was located. It was really spacious. There were two twin-size beds, a TV, and a radio. There were two piles of clothes and toiletries placed on the beds.

"So, how was your ride?" she asked, leaning against the wall.

"It was alright," Jerry said, looking at me.

"I liked the lights and the big buildings," I said, knowing why he was looking at me that way. I made sure I didn't mention anything about our adventure getting to the States.

"How's your mother doing?"

"Oh, she's fine. She told us to call her when we arrived."

"Well, don't worry about that now. We'll call her soon. Just hurry and take care of what you have to so I can introduce you to some people," she said and left the room.

I looked at Jerry and watched him dump the bag of money onto the bed. I knew we had a lot of dough, but we never had a chance to count it.

"How much do you think there is?" I asked.

"I don't know, but we'll count it later," he said, putting it under the bed.

"Let's take a shower and change so we can go upstairs," I said.

The music I heard earlier was coming from the back of the house. I noticed there was a bunch of food on a table, and people both young and old were scattered all around. I walked over to where my aunt stood speaking to another woman.

"Hey, auntie," I said.

"Oh, let me introduce you to my coworker, Beatrice," she said, smiling and staring at me intensely.

I gave her a handshake and said, "Hello."

"Beatrice, this is my nephew, David."

"How're you doing?" she said, still holding my hand.

"David, where's your brother?" Aunt Kathy asked, not noticing how this woman was ogling me.

"I don't know. He was with me when I came out," I said, pulling my hand away from Beatrice's grip.

I turned around and found Jerry in a corner, laughing with a pretty girl.

"There he is," I said, walking over to him.

"Boy, what are you doing?" Aunt Kathy asked, smiling.

"This fool was over here trying to mack to me," the girl said, smiling.

The girl looked at me and stopped smiling. She looked back and forth— first at me, then at Jerry, then back to Aunt Kathy.

"Jerry, this is your cousin Lauren," Aunt Kathy said.

I burst out laughing, but I couldn't fault Jerry. Our cousin had some nice curves. She had my aunt's complexion, along with her catlike eyes. Her hair was pulled up in a ponytail with a full bang. If I didn't find out that she was my cousin, I would have probably done the same thing.

"I knew there were two of you, but I didn't realize you guys are twins. Ma, why didn't you tell me they were twins?" she asked my aunt.

Aunt Kathy just shrugged like it was no big deal. She quickly introduced us to a few more people before leaving us on our own.

"Come on, let me show you off to my girls," Lauren said, grabbing our hands.

We walked over to a group that was laughing and having a good time. Once we got there, one of the girls stopped giggling, and they all turned around to see what stole her attention.

"Ladies, these are the cousins I was telling you about," Lauren said. "Which one of you is Jerry, and which one is David?" she asked, frowning.

We both wore Polo sweaters, blue jeans, and black Timberland boots, so even our clothes were identical.

"I'm David," I said, giving her my best dimpled smile.

"So, this is Jerry's crazy ass," Lauren said, winking at him.

Jerry smiled at the inside joke because he had just been trying to talk to his cousin.

One of the girls stepped forward and said, "I'm Shante," while looking me up and down. Shante was dark skinned and a little on the heavy side.

"Get your wild ass back over there," Lauren said, grinning.

"What's your name, pretty lady?" Jerry asked one of Lauren's friends.

"The girl blushed and answered, "Kara."

Kara had a short haircut and reminded me of the actress Halle Berry. Then the last girl from the group came over and shook my hand.

"Hi, David. I'm Britney," she said, shaking her hair away from her face.

Apparently Britney was a white girl with a ghetto attitude and a body to match. She reminded me of that woman Coco, actor Ice-T's wife, who I once saw in a magazine.

"How do we tell y'all apart?" Shante asked, seemingly confused.

"That would be something for you to find out," Jerry said, looking over at Kara.

"Anyway, how old are you?" Lauren asked, changing the subject.

"Seventeen, until the twenty-fourth of January," I said.

"Tomorrow we're gonna go shopping on the Ave," she said.

"Jerry, David, come over here for a second," Aunt Kathy said, beckoning us.

"Well, it was nice meeting you, ladies," I said.

"You damn right," Britney said, smiling.

"We'll be seeing you again soon," Jerry said.

We left to let them talk among themselves and I glanced back in their direction one last time.

"Dem niggas is fine, and I need to get my ass to Haiti," I overheard one of them saying.

I laughed to myself thinking, *I'm gonna like it here.*

11

Jerry

The following morning, I woke up early since I really couldn't sleep. I turned over in my bed when I heard noises in the kitchen and decided to go upstairs and see who was up. I found Aunt Kathy preparing a pot of coffee, which I would later realize was part of her daily routine.

"Good morning, sweetie," Aunt Kathy said.

"Morning, Auntie," I responded.

"I'm about to head out to work. There's coffee on the stove if you like and bread on top of the fridge. If you want something a little heavier, I can have Lauren fix you some eggs and sausages," Aunt Kathy said, pouring coffee into her cup.

"Don't worry, Auntie, I'll eat cereal this morning," I said, looking into the refrigerator for some milk.

"Okay, sweetie, I will see you later," she said, walking out of the kitchen.

Aunt Kathy had already had some identification papers made up for us. Our first names remained the same, but our last name changed to Benton. Aunt Kathy was now our mother and Lauren, our sister. Later, our Aunt Kathy was going to enroll us in a school called Satellite Learning Center, located on Hillside Avenue. She said it would be the best school for us to get our GEDs. Our main concern though, was to find a way to make some money so we could get Loria and my mother over here safely.

We counted the money the morning after we arrived. We had over one hundred thousand left, since we took twelve grand with us for shopping. The clothes Lauren had us buy were expensive. We had designer names like Coogi, Polo, Moschino, Iceberg, and Tommy Hilfiger.

I was feeling all the attention we were getting, especially from the women who couldn't seem to get enough of us.

Lauren's excuse for buying all this stuff was, "Y'all ain't gonna be looking like some bum-ass niggas in my house." She kept rambling something about being fly and ballas, when some dude suddenly walked up behind her and grabbed her by the waist. I was about to say something, until she turned around and kissed him. I glanced at David, who like me, was wondering who this dude was.

"I want y'all to meet my boyfriend, Zoo," she said, smiling and showing all her teeth.

We both nodded to him.

"What up, niggas?" he said, grinning.

Zoo was slim with braids. He was black as night, had big diamond earrings in each ear, and was wearing a big gold chain that touched his stomach.

"So, these are the cats that are straight off the boat and shit?" he said, laughing.

I wondered what David was thinking, and I instantly didn't like Zoo.

When Lauren had walked in on us counting the money, we told her a watered-down version of what really happened. We told her we had committed a few robberies before coming to the States. Still, I couldn't figure out what role this dude would be playing in our lives and why Lauren even wanted us to meet him.

"Yeah, and what?" I said, sizing him up.

"Ain't shit. I just thought y'all would look different, that's all," he said, still grinning.

I just stared at him and didn't reply. David didn't respond either.

"Um, y'all ready?" Lauren asked, trying to divert my attention.

"Yeah," I said, still grilling him.

Although I didn't like him, his ride was hot. It was a black 4x4 truck with shiny rims. The interior was hooked up, too, and I could see from the outside that he had TVs built in the headrest.

"Y'all niggas don't get to see shit like this in Haiti," he boasted.

His car was nice, but I wasn't going to take too many more of his jokes.

"That's not funny, Zoo," Lauren said.

"I was just playing, babe," he said, grinning.

I really wanted to knock that stupid grin off his face.

"I'm gonna take y'all to the club with me tonight and show y'all how we party in New York," Zoo said excitedly.

I really wanted to say, "Fuck you and that club," but since it was Lauren's boyfriend, I held back.

"Yeah, whatever." I said, as David and I climbed into the back.

12

David

The entire ride to the club with Zoo was very informative. This dude just couldn't stop talking about himself, and I was right there soaking it all in. Jerry looked like he was getting annoyed at having to listen to the constant chatter. I still had no idea what Lauren saw in Zoo, but I was chilling. We all were high as hell. We were in his truck smoking, parked on a side block near the club. I accidentally burned his leather seat in the back, but I didn't care.

"Tonight, we're gonna be in the V.I.P. section, poppin' bottles and shit, feel me? Niggas like us ain't gon' be waiting on line with corny ass cats and all that," he said, blowing smoke.

"What's a V.I.P. section?" I asked.

He cocked his head back and laughed.

"Very Important People getting Very Important Pussy," he said, enunciating the word *pussy* with a sly grin.

"Keep fucking with me, that's gonna become your usual—first-class everything. You feel me. On da real though, how y'all planning to get paper, son?" he quizzed us.

"We don't know yet."

"Alright, cool. I'm gonna put y'all on with me, nah mean?" he remarked, sounding like he was talking to himself more than us.

"To what?" Jerry asked, searching his face for a clue.

"Be easy, son! We gonna talk to y'all about that later. Right about now, it's time to get this shit rocking," he said as he opened the door to get out of the car.

I don't know who the "we" are that he referred to, but I had a
feeling that Jerry and I were going to find out soon.

Outside, the club was crowded with lines that stretched around the
corner. I glanced at the street signs and saw Sutphin and Archer av-
enues. Overhead, I saw a train that looked like it was gliding in the air.
We walked past everyone who was standing in line and stopped in front
of a big black dude who was blocking the entrance. I looked around and
caught some angry glares from the men and noticed some kisses being
blown to me by some of the women. I couldn't help but smile.

"What's up, Zoo?" the big dude asked, moving out of the way.

"Ain't shit, G. Yo, they with me," he said, pointing at us.

"Alright," he said as he lifted the rope and allowed us entry.

Club Mystique was enormous. The first thing I saw once I stepped
inside besides all the people was the big stage filled with guys standing
behind equipment and playing music. The speakers were so huge that I
could feel the bass vibrating in my chest. The women were dressed in
jeans, sneakers, dresses, and skirts, barely hiding anything. We went to
a spot in the club that held very few people. Zoo walked over to a table
and sat next to a dude, who was having a conversation with a nice-
looking woman. I glanced over at Jerry and noticed that his clothes
were glowing from the lights in the club. He was wearing a white-and-
black Enyce zip-up hoodie with a white T-shirt underneath, light blue
jeans, and a pair of Air Force Ones. I looked down at my clothes and
noticed I was glowing as well. The only difference was that the letters
and designs were glowing. I wore the same outfit, but mine had more
black in it, and I wore Timberland boots.

"Come on and sit down. I want to introduce you to someone," Zoo
shouted. "This here is my brother, Black."

I immediately noticed the resemblance. This guy could blend into
the night. He wore a red leather jacket over a black T-shirt with his hat
cocked to the side.

"Which one are you?" he asked, grinning.

I nodded at him and said, "I'm David."

"So, you must be Jerry," he said, looking at Jerry.

Jerry just looked at him and said nothing. I could tell that Jerry didn't like Black either. Whenever he stayed quiet too long, he was either plotting on something or he just didn't like the person.

"Zoo was telling me about you niggas," Black said.

Black waved to a lady who was wearing a short skirt and waved her to come over to us. Jerry just stared at me.

"What y'all drinking?" the lady asked, smiling at me.

"Barbancourt," I said, returning the smile.

She frowned and said, "I'm sorry. I don't know what that is."

I took her hands and pulled her toward me. I whispered in her ear, "It's a top-shelf five-star Haitian rum," then gently brushed my lips against her earlobe.

"Get us three bottles of Alizé, and two bottles of Hennessy," Black said, chuckling.

The lady wrote her number down on a piece of paper and placed it in my hand. She walked away, switching hard.

"Let me find out y'all Haiti niggas got game over there," Zoo said, cheesing.

"We have a lot of things you don't know about," Jerry said, leaning forward in his chair.

"Be easy, homey. Don't pay any mind to this fool over here," Black said.

"But why you so quiet over there? You haven't said much," he said, looking at me.

"I don't speak unless I have to," I said, maintaining eye contact.

No one said anything for a while.

"I like y'all. Y'all look hungry," he said, bobbing his head to the music.

"Yo, this is my shit!" Zoo said, getting up.

He grabbed a random girl and went into the crowd.

"Don't pay him any mind, son. He just plays too much, but fuck all that. I might have a proposition for you two," Black said.

"What do you do?" I asked him.

He didn't say anything. The lady returned with our bottles. She winked at me before she turned around and sashayed away.

"I run a couple of spots here and there," he said, watching the waitress walk off. "I know why y'all out here. Y'all gonna want some paper. Zoo told me y'all gonna be going to school and shit. That's good. A lot of us don't want to go to school, but for you, that can be good. Y'all become educated and still get some money. That way, motherfuckas will stay out of your business and won't know what y'all do. You see, I got all types of spots, but I need a weed spot. New York is a gold mine for that shit. We gonna have some competition from them Jamaican niggas, but I'll get that taken care of, nah mean?" Black said, pausing long enough to take a shot of his drink.

"I got you, though. We'll have more time to talk about that later. Let's go see what's good with these chicks," he said as he stood up.

I laughed, grabbed a bottle, and together we all walked into the crowd.

On the dance floor, we didn't do much dancing. We basically let the women do all the work. I had this light-skinned girl shaking her ass all over me. The music was a little too fast for me. I had to lean on the wall for support because she kept backing that ass up. Everyone was dancing and yelling out the lyrics to the song. Shorty bent over and put her hands on her thighs and started going down low. The sensation of her ass gyrating against me, while seeing her skirt ride over it was enticing me until I felt someone grab me by the shoulder and push me. I looked over and saw the guy who had just pushed me yelling at the girl I was dancing with. She turned around and walked away. He came toward me and began shouting something about his girl. I looked over his shoulder and saw Jerry heading in our direction, and I felt something wet land on my face. I couldn't believe that this dude spit on me. I cocked my arm back and brought my bottle down, crashing it onto his head. Jerry and I started stomping his head into the floor until I saw someone punch Jerry out of the corner of my eye. I left the dude I was stomping and ran over to help my brother. I picked up a broken piece of the bottle and started slashing every exposed area of his body. Blood spewed everywhere.

He finally back up after I caught him on his cheek and he held his face. Blood poured through his fingers and down his arm. He started yelling and tried to rush me. I sidestepped him, and he ran right into

Jerry who then picked him up high and slammed him down hard. During all of this chaos, I never realized a crowd had formed around us, and the music was no longer playing. I went over to Jerry and pulled him away from dude. When I turned around, the big black dude who had been outside was now looking down at me.

"Yo, G, that's my mans and 'em. Don't worry. We out anyway," Black said with Zoo in tow.

"Don't bring these niggas back here no more!" the bouncer said angrily.

"Alright, then. Yo, come on," Black said, and we bounced.

13

Jerry

I woke up this morning with a serious headache. I don't remember much about last night, except for David and I fighting, and even that was a little vague. Aunt Kathy had to go to work this morning, so she woke us up and told us she left breakfast on the table. David and I were talking about the last couple of days when Lauren walked into the kitchen. Her hair was wrapped, and she wore pajamas. She grabbed some food and sat down at the table to join us.

"Don't stop talking just because I'm here. Keep talking," she said, piling eggs onto her fork. "Mmm, I heard about last night. Y'all just better be careful. Word gets around in the 'hood, you know," she said with a concerned look.

"What's up with Britney?" David asked, changing the subject.

"Boy, what you want with Britney? She's too fast for you, and you don't need a girl like that," she said.

"I do! Give her to me!" I said.

She scrunched her face and said, "Hold up, which one are you? We got to do something about this." She pointed back and forth between us.

David and I just laughed.

"Seriously, how can I tell the difference between y'all?" she asked, folding her arms across her chest.

"I don't know. That's something you'll have to find out on your own. We never thought about that anyway," I said.

"I know now. David is the smooth one, and you're the crazy one," she said, pointing at me.

"Actually, I'm David," I lied.

She looked confused now.

"Don't pay him any mind," David said, laughing at her.

"Boy, you better stop playing with me," she said, smacking the back of my hand.

The phone began to ring.

"I got it!" She jumped up.

"That girl is crazy," I said, laughing to myself. Two minutes later, she came back into the kitchen and sat down.

"That was Zoo. He said he's coming to pick y'all up, so get ready," she said, frowning.

"You alright?" I asked, looking at her with concern.

"Yeah, I'm fine. Just go ahead and have fun. Be careful out there," she said slowly.

"Alright," I said, looking over at David.

"You sure?" David asked.

She looked down and said, "Yeah."

I shrugged and said, "Let me know when you're ready to talk," and walked off.

I threw on my brown snorkel jacket, fitted cap, and my brown, Polo buttoned down faded shirt, dark jeans, and Diesel sneakers. I looked in the mirror and smiled. David was wearing a black-and-white Coogi sweater, black jeans, black Chuckkas, and a black snorkel. I took a thousand dollars from the stash and handed David five hundred. I heard the bell ring and asked David if he was ready.

"Yeah," he said, tucking a gun into his waistband.

Once I got outside, I saw Zoo and Black sitting on a red Benz. *I have to get me a car,* I thought.

"How you like this whip right here?" Zoo asked.

"Whip?" David asked, looking at me.

"Yeah, nigga, a whip is a car. This is my cherry S500. One of y'all burnt holes in my seat last night, so I had to pull my baby out 'til I get the other one fixed," Zoo said.

"Enough with the small talk, I got something to show y'all," Black said, getting into the car.

The tan leather interior felt soft as butter and smelled new. The car also had a TV, along with a booming sound system. The ride was smooth and short. We stopped on 161st Street and 89th Avenue. A shelter housing women and their children was on one side, and there was also a big building there, located between a parking lot and a red building that we later learned housed crazy people.

"This is one of my spots. I'm gonna introduce you to a couple of cats right quick," Black said, stepping out of the car.

He went in front of the large building where five guys stood.

"What up, Black?" a skinny dude with dreads greeted.

"What's up? This is my dude, Trigga," Black said. "This here is my boy, Loco," He pointed to a Spanish dude with braids.

"I don't know the rest of these cats, but I guess they live here," Black said, pointing at the other dudes who were leaning against a fence nearby.

"This is my nigga, King," he said, pointing at me. And this here is Major," he said and pointed to David.

David and I glanced at each other without saying a word.

"They good, nah mean. Y'all gonna be seeing a lot of them over time. So y'all gonna get to know each other. But for right now, we gon' take this walk."

We headed toward the parking lot and stopped in front of a little house that was hidden between the building and the parking lot.

"As soon as I get things in order, this is gonna be yours to run. See, I knew I was gonna like y'all as soon as we met. And that scuffle y'all had at the club was crazy. I liked how y'all held it down," he said, laughing. "Anyway, let's take a walk to the store."

We walked toward Hillside Avenue and stopped in front of a car dealership.

"What type of car is that?" I asked Black, pointing at a black coupe.

"That's a Beamer. Trust me, fuck with me, y'all gonna get more than that," he said.

Black is a funny dude because whether we fuck with him or not I was going to get that Beamer.

14

David

Last night, we tried to call our mother but didn't get an answer. In Haiti, a phone is a luxury that not everyone can afford. Our mother has a family friend who owns a photography studio, and once a month on the second Saturday, she should be expecting our phone call. This was the longest time we had ever spent apart from one another. I missed her like hell. But today was our birthday, and we had a lot to do.

Yesterday, Jerry and I decided to treat ourselves to a car. We went back to the dealership on Hillside Avenue. Since we were paying cash, he gave us a great deal. We bought two 1998 three-series BMWs. He also had a connection with an owner of a body shop and hooked us up with a new paint job and rims. We were supposed to pick up the cars today so we could head to a party tonight being held on Lauren's campus at Old Westbury in Long Island.

Doing all that running around with Black, we barely had time to handle any of our own personal business. He drove us around and showed us different spots on South Road, Queens Bridge, and East New York, Brooklyn. We also had to get used to our new nicknames. Black explained we needed aliases in this business, due to all of the snitching and grimy dudes. We also brought cell phones and were now set.

"What's up, Jimmy?" I said, shaking the dealer's hand.

Jimmy was a short, chubby white guy who was going bald but still holding on to the last few strands of hair he had left. He was cool with us since he gave us such a good deal.

"Hey! There go my boys," he said.

"How we looking today?" Jerry asked glancing around the show-room

"Oh, everything's in order. In fact, there are your cars." He smiled and pointed behind us.

When we turned around, I couldn't help but have a huge joker grin on my face. I spotted a midnight blue coupe and a money green one. I quickly walked over to the green car, while Jerry moved toward the blue Beamer. They both had the same package—flip TV screens in the front, a booming sound system, leather interior, mirror-tinted windows, and chrome foot pedals.

"Just because you're my boys, I threw something extra in it for you. Open your glove compartments," he said, grinning.

When I popped open the compartment, I immediately saw a white envelope.

"Go ahead and open it," he said.

When I did, I saw a driver's license, complete with my picture and name on it.

"Good looking out, man!" Jerry shouted from his car.

"No problem. Just make sure you always do business with me. You know what I'm saying," he said with a wink. "I'll always take good care of you guys."

In between signing the bill of sale, he confessed he smoked a lot of weed and had some other wealthy friends who could also be potential customers.

"No problem," I said, thinking about our side hustle with Zoo. "We'll definitely keep in touch."

"See ya later, fellas," he said, watching us pull off.

My phone rang. It was Zoo.

"Yo what's up," I said, stopping at a light.

"Where y'all at?" he asked.

"We're on Hillside."

"Cool. Stop by the spot right quick. I've got something to show y'all."

"Okay," I said, hanging up.

We made a full circle around the block and ended up on 161st Street.

That block always had people on it. I saw Zoo's Benz and pulled up behind him blasting my Haitian music, and Jerry pulled up behind me.

"I see y'all niggas are getting accustomed to this shit. What the fuck is that you niggas are bumping? This is America!" he said, bursting out laughing.

"What you want, man?" Jerry asked, getting annoyed.

Zoo sensed Jerry didn't like him, so there was tension in the air.

"Chill, Jerry, you know I'm fucking around. Follow me," he said.

He pushed open the gate in front of the little house that was hidden between the parking lot and the building. Three dudes were sitting on the porch smoking.

"This is Major and King. These are the dudes that's gonna be running this here," Zoo said, introducing us to the guys who were smoking.

We all nodded at one another.

"Come on, let's go inside."

The house had been abandoned for years, although I could see that Zoo had tried to fix it up a little. The first floor had a dining room and a kitchen. He took us upstairs to a room. Inside, there was a long picnic-style table with a bunch of weed and scales on it.

"There's fifty pounds of haze over there, going for $350 an ounce, and $5,600 a pound. Altogether that's $280,000. Black said he wants $150,000 back. He knows you're gonna need workers and have to pay them, so he's leaving that up to y'all to find them. Y'all cool with that?"

"Yeah, that's cool," Jerry said.

"That's cool," I said.

"Dem niggas out front gonna be watching this till y'all ready. Just give us a call and let us know, alright?" he said, giving us dap to seal the deal.

"How y'all get them whips, anyway?" he asked.

Jerry and I looked at each other and I said, "Birthday gifts," with large grins. We didn't want Zoo knowing we had any type of bread because we know how envious niggas can be.

"Word. That's what I'm talking about, man," he said, giving dap.

I grabbed a bag off the table and put a pound in it.

"We'll holla back later," I said and left.

While getting into the car, I called Lauren.

"Hello," she answered.

"What's up?"

"Where y'all at?" she asked.

"I'm on my way home, and you?"

"I'm on the porch with Britney and Kara, chilling. You still going, right? she asked, referring back to the party.

I heard Britney in the background, saying, "They better," and Lauren laughed.

"Shut up, y'all. Anyway, who's bringing y'all home?" Lauren said.

"Don't worry about that. Just be home, okay?" I joked.

"Alright, gangsta. One," she said, laughing and hung up the phone.

Once I turned the corner, I saw them on the porch. We parked in front of the house and got out of the cars.

Lauren screamed and damn near flew off the porch.

"Whose cars are those?" she asked.

"None of your business," Jerry joked.

"Shut up, Jerry. I know they're not yours," she said.

"Yeah, we got them today. You like them?" I asked.

"Hell yeah, they are hot," Britney said, stepping off the porch.

"What time are y'all leaving?" I asked.

"Whenever y'all ready," Lauren said.

"Alright, we gonna change clothes. Just go get some Dutches while we're getting ready," I said, heading inside.

"Let's get this party started right," Britney said as we entered the house.

I stepped outside with a green Celtics throwback, faded sky-blue Roc-A-Wear jeans, and green-and-white Air Force Ones, matching my whip. Jerry was rocking a dark blue silk Iceberg button down with black slacks and his Diesel shoes. We had gotten our ears pierced, so we had diamond studs, and 360 waves spinning in on our heads.

We were ready to rock the party! We had no problem picking up the American culture and slang. Aside from our accents, we were fitting in quickly.

"Mmm-mmm, y'all niggas are fine," Britney said, licking her lips.

"I might have to watch y'all tonight," Lauren said, laughing.

"Don't worry. We'll be alright," I said.

"I'm rolling with you tonight," Kara said, grabbing Jerry's hand.

"We out then?" he asked.

"Hell yeah," they sang.

Britney got into the car with me, while Lauren and Kara rode with Jerry, pulling up next to me and wanting me to follow them. When we got to the Long Island Expressway, Britney started to play with my zipper.

"Keep driving," she instructed.

I was hard before she even unzipped my jeans. She pulled out my joint and started to massage the head. I adjusted my seat back a little to get more comfortable. She leaned over and started to bob her head up and down. I didn't even realize I was speeding until I was side by side with Jerry's car. I looked over and saw Jerry. Lauren and Kara started waving frantically and mouthed words that I couldn't understand. I nodded and let them pass me. My heart felt like it was about to explode out of my chest as Britney worked her magic. Her head game was ridiculous. I didn't even realize I had closed my eyes until I heard a car honking. I couldn't believe I was swerving into the next lane. I started to shake, and that's when I held her head down with one hand and nutted in Britney's mouth. She zipped my jeans, got up, and wiped her mouth, and then sang, "Happy Birthday!"

I pulled up in front of Lauren's school and waited for Jerry to pull up alongside me. Lauren let down her window and said, "Follow us. The party is in one of the facilities in the back of the campus. And oh, Britney, did you find what you were looking for in David's lap?"

Everyone burst into laughter.

"As a matter of fact, I did!" Britney said, licking her lips.

"Uhhh, you so nasty," Kara said, giggling while letting up her window.

Jerry pulled off, and I followed. The road leading to the campus was dark, narrow, and long. It took us ten minutes to get to the building. I knew we were getting closer and couldn't wait to party. I saw groups of women walking and wearing skimpy outfits, and I heard music coming from a distance. We parked our cars in the student parking lot and walked over to the party. The music was bumping, and the crowd was alive. The women were looking good with a capital "G." Jerry and I tried to ditch the girls, but Britney wasn't going to let me out of her sight. Every time I would try to disappear to one side of the party to get my groove on, she would just happen to pop up out of nowhere. Jerry made fun of me the entire night. Kara was constantly trying to get his attention, but he wasn't really feeling her. He danced with her twice, after making his rounds throughout the party. He left the party with at least five phone numbers. The party ended around three o'clock in the morning, but people were still wired and still wanted to party. One of Lauren's home girls was having an after party in her dorm, and we ended up going there. The rooms were nothing like I expected; they were small and narrow, giving you just enough space for two beds and maybe a computer desk and a closet to store clothes. There were about ten of us in her room, and we played strip poker and truth or dare. We didn't get home until six-thirty in the morning.

15

Aunt Kathy

The twins have adjusted to their new environment quickly, Aunt Kathy thought. When they first arrived she could barely believe her eyes. Although it had been nearly eighteen years, it still felt like it was only yesterday. Aunt Kathy was aware of the fact that Lauren introduced the twins to her boyfriend, whom she didn't have much regard for. Zoo had been showing them around town, and they were hanging out together very often lately, but she was happy they seemed to be fitting right into American culture.

Aunt Kathy left Haiti for two reasons: to pursue a better life and because she was pregnant. After her father found out her sister Barbara was pregnant, he became very upset and cursed the day she was born. He felt Barbara was too young to have a child and hated the fact that she was throwing her life away at the tender age of sixteen. He couldn't stand the sight of Barbara and Reginald, the twins' father together. At the time, Kathy was already four months pregnant with Lauren, so after watching her father behave badly toward Barbara she felt it best to delay telling him. Finally their father set a plan in motion for both daughters to leave Haiti for the United States. Kathy knew the moment he told Barbara of his plan she wasn't going to go for it. However, Kathy didn't have such attachments with her boyfriend. He had already expressed he didn't want any part of their baby.

Barbara was an entirely different story. Barbara breathed Reginald, and in return, he treated her like royalty. Kathy was hurt to know Barbara didn't want to leave, but they promised each other they would always stay in contact. Years later after Kathy was settled, had obtained her degree and began working as a nurse, she made sure to send money home monthly. She was proud when she learned Barbara and Reginald had already opened their own restaurant even before she was able to help out. When they were little girls, Barbara loved to cook, and she was good at it. Unfortunately, one bad thing happened after the next. First Reginald dies suddenly, but at least they still had some means of income. Then years later some hoodlums burned her store down, and it crushed Kathy's heart because she too had some financial issues and was unable to help her sister rebuild. The I.R.S. was threatening to auction off her house, due to all the back taxes. Fortunately, she was able to work out a payment plan and she received a promotion to head nurse, which came with a sizeable raise.

Kathy hadn't spoken to her sister since the arrival of the boys and thought it was time she reached out to her. Barbara should be expecting her call, so she called Photo Lurdes, a photography studio, owned by a friend of the family. He had access to all the latest technologies available in Haiti, and he would often allow people the use of the phones.

"Hello, Lurdes, Sak Pase," Kathy greeted him.

"Hello, Kathy," he responded in a wary voice.

Lurdes explained how her sister's home had been burned down. It was practically disintegrated and there was nothing left but charred dust.

Kathy felt her entire world collapsing around her. *This has to be a bad dream,* she thought.

"Burned down?" she shrieked, almost falling off the bed.

"Yes," Lurdes said barely audible.

"No, no, no!" she shouted as tears filled her eyes. "God, why is this happening? How did this happen? Was there any sign of my sister and her family?"

"There were no signs of life, but there's a slight chance she may have made it out. If she did, no one has seen her, Loria or Johnny since."

"How could this be? Oh Lord, please let my sister be alive. Please," Kathy begged.

"The police are still investigating. So far they've said it looks like someone may have done this intentionally. But they have no leads yet."

Kathy dropped the phone. A million questions ran through her mind, without any answers. She dropped to her knees, and cried all night long. She had no idea what to do. Even more important, how in the world was she going to tell the boys that their family may be dead? For now, she would keep it to herself.

16

Jerry

Our school is off the chain, and we've been there for a few months now. Aunt Kathy enrolled us in the Satellite Learning Center, located on Hillside Avenue and 163rd Street. We'd only been there for a short time, and we already had a squad of Haitians rolling with us. We were the most popular guys in our school, and the girls loved us. There were even a few teachers trying to get with us on the low. The school was nothing like we expected. Schools in Haiti were much stricter, and we had to wear uniforms. We were not allowed to hang out in the hallways, and we definitely weren't able to talk back to the teachers or principals. This here was like a hang-out spot for us to socialize and attend classes. Let's not even mention what some of the girls wore to school. I was in heaven.

We had a lot of business to handle. We were going to open up shop this week and had to break it down to the clique today. We recruited a few Haitian guys from school, and we were supposed to meet at the stash house afterward. We'd been hanging with these dudes for a little while now, and they seemed hungry to get that money. Most of all, they seemed trustworthy, and David thought it was a plus that they were all Haitian.

"Let's keep this money in the family, if you know what I mean," he said.

The school bell rang, and all the students dispersed. As I was picking up my book bag, Mrs. Kelly stepped in front of my desk. Mrs. Kelly was the math teacher, and she was bad, especially for an older woman.

"When are you going to stop messing with these little girls and get with a real woman?" she asked in a seductive voice.

Mrs. Kelly is a dime for real. She is the spitting image of the actress LisaRaye, except she had shorter hair.

"Whenever you're ready," I said, moving in front of her.

I slid my hand beneath her dress, and she jumped from my bold action, but she didn't stop me and I continued. Gently, I slid my fingers toward her center and rubbed in a circular motion, exciting her. She started to shiver and said, "We're going to get caught."

I grinned and said, "When you're ready to stop dealing with them old niggas, give me a call." I removed my hand, licked my fingers, and walked away.

My car was parked in front of the stash house since it was only two blocks away from school. When I reached the spot, I saw Rockhead and Smitty holding the front down.

"What's good, King," Smitty said, giving me dap.

"What's up?"

"Major and 'em niggas are inside already," he said.

"Good looking out," I said and walked inside.

I saw David sitting at the round table, talking to everyone around him. There were six of us: Block, Jinx, Bones, Ricky, David, and myself. Block was a real rider, down-for-whatever type of dude. He was dark skinned and stocky and always wore his hair in a neatly cut afro. Jinx was a short and skinny dude with a major complex. He always thought people were trying to disrespect him. Ricky was tall and fat. He was the quiet dude in the background, always looking like he was plotting. Bones was the skinniest dude out of the whole bunch. He always had something slick to say. We were all Haitians and knew what it really meant to stick together.

"What's up?" I said, giving dap to everyone.

"Ain't shit," Bones said, passing a blunt.

I took a couple of pulls and passed it off.

"You're ready?" David asked me.

I nodded and took a seat.

"Alright, today is the beginning of the biggest Haitian movement these motherfuckers will ever see. King and I are going to make sure everybody eats. We all know what it's like to be fucked up and starving. Today is the end of all that shit. There is no *I* in *Us*. Whatever King and I got is for the team. That's the kind of attitude we'll have from here on out. There will be no fighting between Haitians. That shit is dead. If you got something to say about someone or feel some way, then this is the place to speak your mind. There will be no public disputes whatsoever. Doing so will result in a ten percent deduction from your pay. The percentage will rise with further violations until it leads to permanent termination. We'll all do something productive with our time and image in order to keep everyone out of our business. You either go to school or have a job. Since we're all in school, I expect y'all to keep your grades up. We won't talk or brag about our money or our business to outsiders. We are not drug dealers, we are businessmen. We will use our cell phones to remain in contact with one another, especially when we're out conducting business. We all should have an emergency contact in case an urgent situation occurs. With that being said, I'm going to pass it off to King."

I got up when he stopped talking and paced as I spoke. "We should be expecting shipments from Black every fourteen to twenty-one days. On the day of the drop-off, one of us will be present. We'll rotate positions for every drop-off. We'll install cameras within the coming week. Nobody other than the people here right now should be in this house. I suggest we have a rainy day stash. That's important. The money we get will be split evenly. Right now, we have forty-nine pounds of haze. Black wants $150,000 of every $280,000 he fronts us. Being that there are six of us, Major and I will put up the first fifty grand to get us started. That's our gift to you. Bones and Ricky will be in charge of security. Block and Jinx will be in charge of the money going in and out. Once a month, we'll have a meeting. Before I end this segment, I want to bring something else to your attention. In this instance, we are now working for Black. I want you to know there are no leaders in this community, so, working for this nigga will not be our life. Major and I have been running some ideas past each other, and I know for certain we'll be venturing out in order to become independent. In the near future, when the time presents itself, we'll let you know of our plans. I don't know if this dude will be happy about us leaving him, but just to make sure, I want to be ready, if and when he decides to go to war. Bones and Ricky, I need you to find out as much as you can about this dude—where he sleeps, eats, and shits. That's it for now, so if you have any questions or anything to say, speak now or forever hold your peace," I said, looking at everyone.

Nobody said anything until Bones raised his hand.

"Yeah, I got something to motherfucking say. Why this fat nigga Ricky always quiet? Every time he gets hungry, he looks at me like I'm a bucket of chicken. I think that nigga wanna eat me, yo," he said, making everyone laugh.

"Shut up, nigga," Ricky said, joining in the laughter.

"Alright, then. Since everyone understands, let the games begin. We're gonna show one another nothing but love and the utmost respect. Haitians4Life!" David shouted as he stood up.

"Haitians4Life!" everyone responded.

"Now spark up," I said, sitting down, and we continued to chill, like we've been boys for years.

17

Jerry

We'd been running the drug spot for a couple of months, and business was booming. We make about fifteen grand a week, after breaking Zoo and Black off with their cut. Product had been moving fast. We stuck to selling weight only, no nickel and dime bags for us. We had clientele all over the city, and we didn't discriminate. Jinx got Flatbush and Jamaica Avenue locked down. Bones had Hollis and East New York, while Ricky had Hempstead on lock. Plus, Block had been staking his claim up in Harlem. They were giving him problems at first, but after a little persuasion, things fell into place.

We had to set up a meeting with Tony Sanchez, one of the top dogs in Harlem. We let Sanchez peoples know we had the best product around, and at a good price. The Jamaican dudes who we were in competition with didn't appreciate it when we stepped into their territory. They followed Block one night while he was making a drop and tried to stick him up. Luckily, Block had Ricky and Jinx follow him that night because he was going outside his hood. They approached Block as he was getting out of the car. One of the dudes hit him in the back of the head with the butt of his gun while the other guy started searching the car for whatever else he could find. As soon as Jinx saw what was going on, he ran up behind the dude and hit him across the face with a crowbar. Block was still on the floor holding the back of his head. Jinx continued stomping the shit out of the Jamaican dude while Ricky focused his attention on the other guy. He pulled out his gun and told him to get the fuck out of the car and lay down on the ground. Block got up and started kicking him in the face with his boots. After pounding him to the ground, they took their car and whatever money they had on them and left all of them lying in the street fucked up. That was the last time we heard from that crew.

Jerry and I tried not to deal directly with the customers. There were only three people we made the exception for, and that's because they were high-profile clients. Jimmy from the car dealership only wanted to deal with Jerry or me, and since he hooked us up with other big spenders, we did him that solid. We tried telling him that everyone in the crew was cool, but he insisted on only dealing with us. He usually bought three to four ounces at a time and always asked us if we wanted to chill out and smoke with him.

Preston Jones was the city councilman for the district from Brooklyn and was our other client. He called us twice a month and bought an ounce of the exotic shit, Kush, Haze, or Sour Diesel, which could cost almost $700. He would usually have his bodyguard meet us at a diner or a strip mall somewhere outside the city, in order to pick up the product. We didn't mind going out of our way because we knew one day we might need a favor from him. Also, in return for keeping his secret, he hits us off with a nice bonus.

Then there is Kim Lew aka The Biggest Threat, and she was a prominent and successful real estate/architect business owner. She had buildings all over the United States, including seven major ones in New York City. She was always in the media for her controversial and lavish lifestyle, and we met her through Jimmy. They called her the Biggest Threat because she would not hesitate to rip the rug out from under your feet while you were still standing. She definitely was a cutthroat businesswoman, but she looked good doing it. She would call us every Friday before heading off to her weekend of nonstop partying. Once, she invited us to one of her parties, and I will say is it was definitely an experience worth remembering. They were doing everything—from popping pills to eating mushrooms and taking shots of 150-proof liquor. People were on the back patio having orgies, while others watched and videotaped. We didn't get involved with all the other stuff. We just stuck to what we knew, which was smoking weed, fucking and drinking liquor. Jerry and I left after smashing these two white freaks by the poolside, but we were invited to party all weekend. We hadn't been back since, but were planning to return.

I walked into the stash house and noticed Jerry sitting at the table rolling up.

"What's good, son?" I asked him, noticing something was bothering him.

"Nothing much. I was just sitting here, thinking about making our move away from Zoo and Black. We're losing money," Jerry said.

"Yeah, man, I was thinking about that shit, too. I was waiting for the fellows to get back to us with the information on Black and Zoo. Once we have that leverage, we can go through with our plans to leave," I said.

"We got the basic info, like where he lives and where his shawty rest at, but we need more. We need to know where his people lay their heads and who else besides the Jamaicans, he got beefs with," Jerry said, sparking a blunt.

"I'm gonna ask Jinx if he heard anything else from his man, but we can't wait forever, so we're gonna have to set our plan in motion soon," I said, taking a few pulls from the blunt.

"For real, man, let's set our plan in motion. We just need to find the perfect opportunity," Jerry said.

18

Jerry

David and I were in the backyard smoking and reminiscing, and I couldn't help but wonder what was going on in Haiti. It had been months since we spoke to our family, and I'd been thinking about them a lot lately. I didn't know about David, but I had been having bad dreams for the past week. Like last night, I dreamt I saw Lori bleeding and crying for me in some back alley. She was yelling and reaching out for me, but every time I got closer to her, it was like she moved farther away, until she was no longer there. All I could hear was her screaming. The last time I asked Aunt Kathy if she had spoken to my mom or brother, she just said, "No," and that she had people checking up on them.

"You heard what I said?" David asked, looking at me.

"Nah. I was zoning out a little bit. I'm high as a motha—"

"I said, I met this girl last month on Farmer's Boulevard while I was driving around. She reminded me of Fifi. I miss her and I've been thinking about her. When we get things in order I'm gonna send for her. Yeah, I think I'm gonna do that," he said, looking like he was day-dreaming.

I totally forgot about that bitch. And now, thinking about it, I was wondering what ever happened to her. I never even told my brother about what went down that night. I knew this nigga was going start crying about it.

"Aye, listen, man, I got some—"

"Yo, you hear that?" David said, getting out of his seat.

"It sounded like crying."

"Is Aunt Kathy home?" I asked.

"Nah. She went out with her friend," he said.

We got up and started creeping toward the house door. The closer we got, the louder the noise became. I heard shouting, too. I motioned to David to follow me, and I stopped at the inside door. I looked in and saw Lauren on the floor, crying, with blood spewing from the side of her mouth.

"Please, baby, stop it! You're hurting me!" she pleaded.

"What I tell you about not picking up your phone, huh!" Zoo shouted, sounding drunk, then he smacked her causing her to sob loudly.

"I'm trying to tell you that my battery died. You know I would've called you, baby."

"Shut up, bitch! Stop lying!" he yelled.

"I'm going in there," David whispered into my ear.

I placed my arm out and stopped him, then I wiggled my finger, telling him to follow me. We ran down to the side of the house and opened the gate.

We got to the front and spotted Zoo's car doors unlocked. We got into the backseat of his truck and lay low, waiting for him to come out.

Thirty minutes later, we heard the house door rattle as if it were going to come off its hinges. We heard him get into the car and slam the door. He pulled out his phone and dialed some numbers, then asked for someone by the name of Shelly.

"What's up, Shelly? You know who this is, man. Stop playing. That nigga ain't there, is he? Cool. Have something sexy on, and I'll be there in about an hour. One!" he said, hanging up the phone.

He started the car and took off. I knew the area like the back of my hand. He was going to take a curve and slow down for a speed bump. I felt the car slowing down and looked over at David. I signaled to him that I was about to make my move, and as soon as the car took the curve and was about to slow down, I popped up and pushed the gun to his head.

"Stop the fucking car now!" I yelled and felt the car jerk.

"What the fuck is this about?" Zoo asked, looking into the rearview mirror. "Oh, it's y'all niggas. Is this a fucking joke or something?"

"You heard what he fucking said!" David yelled, rising up from the backseat.

"This isn't a fucking joke. Put the car in park and put your hands behind your head!" I repeated.

"I don't know who y'all think y'all fucking with, but wait 'til I get out of this car," Zoo said, doing what I asked.

I hit him in the back of the head with the butt of my gun, letting him know we weren't playing.

"Ahhh!" Zoo yelled. "Y'all niggas just sealed y'all coffins."

"Get the fuck out of the car—now!" David yelled as he exited the back door.

David opened the front door to let Zoo out of the car. As soon as Zoo got out, he charged David, knocking him off balance. David stumbled a little, then he grabbed Zoo by the back of his tee shirt, causing it to rip and slip out of his hand. I got out of the car as soon as I saw Zoo trying to make a run for it and chased after him. He ended up running about three cars down before David picked up an object off the ground and threw it, hitting him in the back. Zoo lost his footing and fell to the ground. As he tried to get up, I ran behind him and kicked him in the stomach. David followed me and started punching and kicking him in the face.

"This is for making us chase your stupid ass!" David spat.

"Now, we got to drag this fucker to the car and put him in the truck," I said.

"No we don't. Make this nigga walk. He had enough strength to run down here, he has enough strength to walk to the car," David said.

Zoo was on the ground, groaning from the pain. He looked up at us and said, "What's wrong with y'all niggas?"

"Learn to keep your fucking hands to yourself, nigga," I spat.

"What you talking about?" Zoo asked, looking confused.

"My sister," I answered.

"Yo, you know I didn't mean anything by that shit, man. We just had a little misunderstanding," Zoo tried to explain.

"Whatever, nigga. Get your ass off the ground and walk to the fucking car," I said with my gun jammed in his back.

Zoo got up, and we walked to the car. Zoo and I climbed into the back while David drove.

"Let's bring him to the spot and let the fellows in on our new endeavor," I said, speaking in Creole to David. "I think we just found our second occupation."

19

David

Today, my niggas, is the day we've been waiting for," Jerry said. "First and foremost, I would like to say that I appreciate the loyalty and dedication you guys have put forth. The last six months couldn't have gone any better. The time we've donated to our business ventures has been rewarding. Everyone in this room has accumulated well over $200,000 apiece. The monthly reports given to us by Block and Jinx account for all the money flowing, making sure there are no problems. As I stated before, drug dealing will not be a permanent fixture in our future. Today is the day. Before I go any further, I would like to say that if anyone objects to this, don't be afraid to voice your opinion. I must warn you that what we are about to get into is not considered a game. If you don't have the heart to ride for the cause of money and power, then you're in the wrong house. If you wish to leave, then this is the time. No hard feelings will be harbored against you, but if you decide to leave in the midst of this meeting, then your decision will become detrimental. So, I'm going to ask once more, who wants out?" Jerry asked, looking everyone squarely in the eye.

No one got up, and Jerry had commanded everyone's full attention.

"Good. Then, I'm going to pass it off to Major to elaborate on the specifics," Jerry said, taking a seat.

"King and I have been passing this idea back and forth between the both of us for some time now. We've come to the conclusion that this mission guarantees three things—death, jail or wealth, depending on the circumstances. I don't know about any of you, but I choose wealth. Never in America has there ever been an organization this grand that is solely dedicated to this profession." I paused for a grand effect.

"In Haiti, we already know that robbery, murder, and extortion are as regular as walking to the corner store, but what we are about to unleash in America borders on terror. We are about to make history and begin a new chapter. Your lives will change tremendously after today. What I propose to you gangstas is recognition, money, and infamy. Over the past few months, we've acquired new blood, but after today, there'll be no new faces. Anyone outside of this establishment that gains any knowledge of our true purpose will be subjected to physical termination," I emphasized.

Ricky raised his hand.

"Yeah, but what is this new project?" he asked.

"Kidnapping," I said, watching everyone carefully.

"Yo, who we plan on snatching?" Ricky asked, looking up from the floor. "'Cause I've seen a few cats out here with money for the taking, nah-I mean?"

"It's about motherfucking time shit got poppin', dog. All this money and shit is cool, but it ain't shit if you ain't making it exciting," Bones said, rubbing his hands together like he was about to eat.

"I'm glad to know you're excited, Bones. I'm also happy to say we already have our first mark," I said, smiling. I paused to let the anxiety build up, then yelled out, "Zoo!"

"Yo, I never liked dude for real," Block said, scrunching his face.

"Yeah, man, son always had some slick shit to say, yo. When we gonna get 'im?" Jinx asked.

"We already have him," I said, grinning. I saw some puzzled faces and said, "It's done."

"So, what we gonna do now?" Block asked.

"Exactly. That's the point of this meeting," I said.

We have to figure out how much ransom we're asking and how

much time we plan on giving Black to come up with the dough. This right here is our first body snatching, and it's personal, because it hits close to home.

"What happened, son?" Ricky asked..

"This motherfucker had the nerve to put his hands on my sister, and I know it wasn't the first time. Pussy-ass nigga!" Jerry responded angrily.

"That bitch-ass nigga did what?" Jinx shouted. "Nah, we not having that. My dad used to hit my moms, and I hated that nigga. Yeah, we gonna teach that nigga a lesson."

"A lesson he'll never forget," I said.

20

Black

Black woke up in a good mood. He was supposed to hook up with his Puerto Rican connect and pick up some product, drop it off and then collect his money. He was planning on making about forty grand from this drop. He arrived at his connect's house to pick up the product, but it was less than what he expected. Black was pissed because he hated when people messed with his money, but he rocked with it anyway. After leaving, he placed a call to confirm the drop-off time. Black usually had Zoo or one of his other soldiers handle the drop-off, but as of lately, he'd been feeling disconnected from the street and wanted to get out and stomp the pavement again.

"Yo, son, what time should I be there?" Black asked, into the phone.

"Yo, son, we may have a problem. Shorty didn't arrive with the loot as scheduled. She said she didn't leave PA until an hour ago," the person on the other line said.

"What? That's bullshit, man. What time was Shorty supposed to arrive 'cause I have business to handle and don't want to sit on this shit all day," Black said, getting annoyed.

"By this afternoon, man."

"A'ight. Later, son," Black said, hanging up.

Black sat back in his seat and thought, *That's why I left this shit up to Zoo and them. Niggas are never on time. I'm gonna stick to giving orders and setting up rendezvous with motherfuckers. After this, I'm gonna give Latoya a call 'cause she knows how to make me feel better.*

Black was on his way to Latoya, his main booty call's house, after a long day of working the streets. His day didn't go as planned, so he was ready to unload and relax. He called to make sure she was home, and also to find out what she wanted from the liquor store. When Black arrived, he found her in the living room, naked and on all fours, waiting for him.

"Hi, daddy. I missed you," she said.

"Oh really, baby girl, and how much?" Black said.

"Come over here and let me show you, daddy."

He walked over to the couch, unbuttoning his shirt and walked out of his pants.

She opened her mouth wide and said, "Ahhhhhh."

Black took a deep breath, tilted his head back, grabbed the back of her head, and enjoyed his welcome-home treatment. He looked down at her and said, "Baby, this is why you're number one."

After a long evening of moving between the living room and bedroom, they were finally worn out. They fell asleep feeling good and tired.

Suddenly, the phone rang.

"Shit," Black said, turning over to answer his cell phone. "Hello."

"Yo, Black, these mother—"

Black sat up in the bed. "Zoo?" he said.

"If you wanna see your brother alive again, make sure you answer the phone the next time I call, and don't let the phone ring more than twice," the caller said, then hung up.

"Who the fuck is this? Do you know who you fuckin' with!" Black yelled, realizing he was talking to no one. "Fuck! Shit! Fuck!" He got dressed.

"Is everything alright, baby?" Latoya asked, leaning on her elbow.

"Yeah, just go back to sleep. I'm gon' get up wit' you later," he said, rushing out the door.

He jumped into his car and started dialing some numbers on his cell phone.

"Hello?" Major said.

"Yo, something's come up. I need y'all niggas to meet me at Kings Park," Black said, pulling off.

"Alright. Is everything good? You need me to call some goons?" Major asked.

"Nah. Just get over here—fast. We can handle this situation solo. One," Black said.

21

David

Jerry and I drove to Kings Park in his car. Kings Park was located on 158th Street, between Jamaica Avenue and 89th Avenue. We spotted Black in the center, pacing in front of a bench. He looked crazy, like he had more than a lot on his mind. His shirt was buttoned the wrong way, and his belt was unbuckled. His zipper was wide open, and his hair was fucked up. We got out of the car and walked over to the park bench.

"What up, Black?" I said, looking him up and down.

"Man, somebody done fucked up and kidnapped Zoo," Black said, still pacing.

"Word? How? You sure?" I asked, feigning surprise.

Black told us about the conversation he had with the mysterious caller.

"Damn. What you gonna do?" Jerry asked, taking a seat on the bench.

"I don't know. All we can do is wait it out. Dem mothafuckers best not touch him, yo," he said, sighing and finally sitting down.

"Did they say anything else? Jerry asked.

"Nah. Just to wait for their phone call."

I could tell he had no idea who was involved, which was the plan.

"Who do you think it is?" I asked curiously.

"I don't know, man. A lot of niggas have been trying to take my spots. All I kn—" His phone began to ring.

"Yo," he said, answering his phone. Jerry whispered to him to put it on speaker.

"Listen up. I'm only going to say this shit once. I don't like echoes, so don't go repeating shit I say. If you even attempt to get stupid on this phone call, don't expect me to call back. For every day I don't get my money, I'll mail a piece of your brother to you. You have three days to give me one million dollars—all hundreds, packed into two duffle bags and divided into ten thousand stacks. You'll receive another phone call with the location." Then the caller hung up.

"Damn, they mean business," I said my voice filled with concern.

"He wants a million in three days, or I'll get my brother mailed to me in pieces. Somebody gonna pay," Black said, wiping his tears away.

"Don't worry, son. We'll get that nigga back. Just go and take care of what you have to, and I'm gonna go make some calls and figure out what's going on," Jerry said.

"Yeah," he said, looking as though his life was over.

"Cool," I replied.

We gave him dap and parted ways.

22

Jerry

I was in Brooklyn, driving on Ocean and Avenue H, heading out to see Mrs. Kelly, my sexy ass math teacher. She called me about an hour ago and asked me to stop by her house. Her building was located on a dead-end street. The street was very quiet with houses lined up on one side and buildings on the other. The address she gave me indicated she lived on the side with the buildings. Someone opened the lobby door, and I proceeded to enter. I dialed her number as I headed toward the elevator bank.

"Hello," a sexy voice answered.

"I'm downstairs in the lobby," I said.

"Take the elevator to the fifth floor," she said.

"Alright," I said and hung up.

The lobby was clean, not like some of the other buildings I'd been to in Brooklyn. I was shocked when I entered the elevators and it did not smell like urine.

I got off on the fifth floor. Opening the door, I realized I didn't get an apartment number.

Glancing to my left, I noticed a door was slightly ajar and walked in that direction. When I got to the door I pushed it opened and walked in.

"Hello, Mrs. Kelly," I said as I entered the apartment

"Come in and lock the door behind you," she replied.

Her apartment was small but cozy. Closing the door, I observed my surroundings, casually taking everything in.

I heard slow music playing in one of the rooms. I followed the sound to what I figured to be her bedroom and opened the door. I smiled when I walked into the room. She was on all fours with her ass facing me. She had one hand between her legs and two fingers gliding in and out of her center as she gyrated to the sounds on the radio. She looked incredible for a woman her age. She had a Coke-bottle shape, perfect sized breasts, a fat ass, and a small waist. Her skin was smooth, with no noticeable stretch marks. As I approached the bed, I watched her sexy ass jiggle as she pleasured herself. She turned on her back and spread her legs to show me her shaved front.

"Hello to you, too," I said, moving toward her.

"I see someone's very happy to see me," she said, looking at my sweatpants.

She dropped my sweats, then she massaged my joint with one hand while playing with herself with the other.

"You ready?" she said in a seductive voice, looking me in the eyes.

She got off the bed and dropped to her knees in front of me. Before I could brace myself, she took my entire manhood into her mouth and started moving back and forth as my dick hit the back of her throat. "Damn," was all I could manage to say as she continued for a while doing tricks with her tongue that I'd never experienced before.

She realized I was about to come and stopped abruptly, wearing a smirk on her face. I didn't appreciate her getting the upper hand on me so quickly. Taking my shirt off, I glanced down and wondered when the hell she put a condom on me.

"You got tricks, huh?" I said, smiling at her.

She chuckled as she moved to the center of the bed. I looked around and noticed a scarf on the dresser. I grabbed it, threw it in her direction, and told her to blindfold herself. I walked out of the room and searched for the kitchen. I went straight to the freezer to grab some ice when I saw a box of Popsicles. I grabbed two and headed back to the room. She was blindfolded now and still playing with herself. I put the cherry-flavored popsicles down and tied her wrists to the bedpost with a pair of stockings that I took from her dresser drawer.

"I got some tricks, too. Where are your CDs?" I asked.

"In the case, near the radio."

I changed the CD, threw on some dancehall Reggae, and started working my magic. I took the Popsicle and rubbed it on her neck until the juices started to run down her chest. I massaged her nipples until she started to tremble and moan uncontrollably. I brought the Popsicle down to her navel and let the juices drip inside. I rubbed the pleasure pop on her thighs, then stopped. I put the rest of the Popsicle in her mouth, and I continued to lick and suck the trail I laid on her. I opened the other package and bit a nice piece off. With my middle finger, I fingered her until I found that soft spongy spot I was looking for. With the Popsicle in my mouth, I licked the letters of the alphabet on her clit while my index and middle finger pleasured her sweet spot. Whenever she tried to move, I followed her until she couldn't anymore.

"What-are-you-doing-to-me?" she bawled out in ecstasy.

I moved on top of her, and she said, "Wait a second!" I untied her and moved her toward the edge of the bed until her feet were on the floor and her stomach was leaning on the mattress. I tied her wrists behind her back and slid slowly inside of her, letting her feel every inch of my hardness. I grabbed her wrists with my left hand and placed my right hand over her shoulder for balance.

"Aw shit," she said, moaning.

Her ass was moving all over the place. I started to lose control, like a robot starting to malfunction. I was smashing her ass so fast, you would have thought someone was applauding.

"Damn, this pussy tight!" I groaned.

"Aw, fuck! Take that pussy! It's yours now, daddy!" she shouted.

I smacked her ass and asked her, "You like that?"

"Yeah, yeah, yeah! Come with me!" she said, coming again.

I untied her wrists and told her to hold my neck as I lifted her up. We went at it like that until we both came in unison. After it was over, we laid on the bed, gasping and trying to catch our breath.

"Are you hungry?" she asked, putting her head on my chest.

"Not for food," I joked.

"You better stop playing," she said and slapped my chest.

"I have to leave in thirty minutes," I said, noticing it was nearly 3:00 A.M.

"Why? You just got here," she said and pleaded for me to stay.

"I have to take care of some business."

"Mmmm, you probably gonna run off to one of your little girlfriends."

"Nah, it's not even like that."

"Then, what business is there?"

"If I tell you, I might have to kill you," I said, half joking. "Anyway, I'm not trying to be here when your husband gets home."

"Fuck him. I can't stand his ass anyway. I'm tired of his bullshit."

"Then why you keep fucking with him?" I asked.

She stayed quiet a little while, then said, "He's all I have. I've been with him since I was seventeen. If it wasn't for him, I probably would have been in a shelter," she said, sounding like she was in a zone.

"Really. How? What happened to you?" I asked. "What do you mean?"

"I'm an only child. My parents died in a car crash when I was sixteen. The state put me in a group home since no one came to claim me. On my seventeenth birthday, I was out with some friends, smoking and drinking, when two police officers asked us for ID. One of them asked me where I lived, and when I explained my situation to him, he began flirting with me, and that was all she wrote. He was turning twenty-five, and after a couple months of dating, he asked me to move in with him. Eventually, we got married."

"Hold up! Your husband's a cop, and you got me in the crib?" I asked in disbelief.

"He won't be home until tomorrow, baby," she said.

"You must be crazy! You got me lounging on his bed with nothing but my boots, and you ain't think to tell me earlier he was a cop?" I said, putting on my clothes, then I walked out of her room and out of the apartment.

"Please, I'm sorry!" she shouted after me.

Good pussy or not, it wasn't worth risking my life for it.

23

Jerry

Back in Queens, I was heading to one of my soldier's cribs on Highland Avenue. I called David, but he was still with a shorty, and I wanted to check on how things were going with Zoo. As I pulled into the driveway, I saw my man Gully in his backyard. Gully is Jinx's cousin. I liked him because he was one of those old-school Haitians who only wore slacks, button front shirts that were ironed to a crisp and dress shoes, no matter what the occasion, and he wasn't afraid to rep his country, unlike some of the Americanized Haitians out here. I gave him dap and followed him down into the basement. When we got there, Zoo was in the middle of the room, still tied to a chair. He looked fucked up from that smack down we gave him the night we brought him here. I walked over to him and smacked him awake.

He yelled through the scarf he had tied around his mouth.

"Look who's up," I said, laughing.

He was trying to say something, so I removed the scarf from his mouth.

"Fuck you, you fucking coconut!" he spat.

I punched him in the mouth.

"Say it again," I dared him. When he didn't respond, I added, "Now, what kind of man puts his hands on a woman, especially one of my family members?"

"Listen, I told you I was drunk, man. It was just a misunderstanding," he pleaded.

I gagged him again and walked away.

"Everything is going as planned. Call Black in two days. I'm gonna make a call and see if that car's ready," I said to Gully.

We copped two additional cars and made a few modifications to them and were now waiting to pick them up.

"Alright," he said and nodded.

"Cool. Call me if anything comes up," I said, giving him dap and left.

David

Last night I had a talk with Lauren when I got home. I found her crying in the backyard.

"What up?" I asked her.

"Black said that someone kidnapped Zoo," she said, wiping away her tears.

I felt bad until I sat down and noticed a bruise under her eye.

"What happened to your eye?"

"I had a fight at school, but I whipped her ass, though."

I stared at Lauren for a while then asked her, "When was the last time you saw Zoo?"

"It's been almost a week."

"Don't worry, everything will be alright," I said, rubbing her back.

After leaving Lauren, I went downstairs to my room. Jerry wasn't home yet, so I decided to smoke a blunt while I waited. "Fuck that nigga, Zoo," I said to myself, all the while thinking about Lauren's eye. "He deserves whatever happens to him."

The next day after school, Jerry and I made plans to go check out Black. While I was walking down the hallway, I stopped by Mrs. Kelly's class to hand in my report since I overslept and missed her class that morning. Class had just ended and no one was there.

"Hi, Mrs. Kelly," I said.

She turned around and smiled.

Before I could say anything, she said, "Listen, Jerry I'm sorry about what happened yesterday. I'm kind of hoping we could start over. What I experienced with you last night was so amazing. I would like for us to be together. I know there's an age difference, but I think we can work it out, if you'll give me a chance."

"I'm not Jerry, I'm David," I said with a smirk, amused at what she just said.

She looked mortified, like her skirt had just gotten caught in her panties, then she cried out, "What?" "Oh my God!" She gasped, covering her mouth.

"Don't worry. Your secret's safe with me, and I'll relay the message."

"I am so sorry," she said, still in shock. "I thought you were your brother since I didn't see him today."

"No problem. Bye, Mrs. Kelly," I said, smiling as I left the classroom.

The bell rang, and everyone started scrambling to get to class. While heading to class, I ran into Block.

"What up?" I asked.

"Yo, we need to have a meeting after school," he said.

"Is it an emergency?" I quizzed

"Hell, yeah."

"Alright then. I'm gonna call my brother and let him know."

"This could be the next big thing," he said, with a wide grin.

"One," I said, giving him pound.

Emergency Meeting

"What's up, Block? Everyone here?" King asked.

"Yo, yesterday I was at the movies on the Ave and ran into this white boy who was poppin' shit to my shorty on the food line, so I pressed him. He was talking all this Big Willy shit, so after the flick, I followed this nigga. Come to find out, he lives in Jamaica Estates, in one of those big houses, so you know this bastard got paper," he said excitedly.

Everyone stayed quiet for a while.

"What do y'all think?" he asked.

"Do you remember where he lives?" Ricky asked.

"I memorized the shit."

"Alright, listen up. If everyone in this room decides this is what they want to do, then we'll go for it. So what's up?" King asked.

"I'm down, "Ricky said.

"I don't care," Jinx said.

"As long as there's money involved, I'm with it," Bones said.

"Alright then. Block is gonna show y'all where this nigga lay his head. We gonna need y'all to scope him out and find out his schedule. Major and I are gonna put together a plan on how to get this paper. Whenever y'all ready to snatch him up, just go for it, but just don't make it hot and hurt him. Y'all already know where to take him."

"Haitians4Life," King said, getting up to end the meeting.

"Haitians4Life!" everyone yelled in unison.

24

David

Jerry and I were back at the stash house. Black asked us to meet him here this morning. With all this shit we had going on, we had to be careful, especially with this dude. He looks like he's going crazy. He still had on the same clothes from when we saw him last, which was two days ago, and he smelled funky. We watched him as we smoked, and he couldn't sit still.

"Dem niggas are supposed to call me today," he said.

"Did you find out who's behind the kidnapping?" I asked.

"Nobody knows nothing, man, and that's the fucked-up shit," Black said.

"Listen, son, King and I wanted to talk to you about something," I said.

He looked at us and said, "What is it?"

"We're gonna help you out with this shit as much as possible, but after that we want out."

"What you mean y'all want out?" he said with a screwed-up face.

"We've been thinking a lot about school, and we're both looking forward to going to college, so we want out of the drug game."

He nodded for a while, like he understood.

"Y'all motherfuckers must think I'm a sucker. I done put y'all niggas on, and after y'all get y'all a little paper, y'all want out!" he shouted.

"Like he said, we're out, so if you can't understand that, then fuck you!" Jerry cosigned.

"If you can handle the fact that we're out after this, then we'll help find Zoo, and then we'll all go about our business," Jerry replied calmly.

He laughed and said, "Y'all niggas think y'all gangsta, huh? Then have it your way."

Jerry and I looked at each other and got up to leave. As we walked out the door, Jerry warned, "Don't try anything stupid with us."

"You're threatening me?" Black asked, steaming.

Jerry shrugged and said, "No, we're just having it your way."

We were on our way back home, and since Aunt Kathy still didn't know that we had whips, we parked a block away from the house. Tonight, we were having a family dinner, which didn't happen very often. Aunt Kathy's work schedule was so hectic that we hardly saw each other anymore. Usually, she'd cook before she left for work, leaving the food on the stove in containers for us. We were now all seated at the kitchen table, having a nice conversation over some good Haitian food. Aunt Kathy hooked it up. She made macaroni pie, sweet plantains, rice and beans, griot, and fried pork shoulder, along with a side of green salad.

"So, how's everything going with school?" She asked us.

"Hopefully, we passed the G.E.D. exam, so we can move on to college," I said, grabbing the bowl of rice.

"Yeah, maybe we'll go to Lauren's college or something," Jerry said, stuffing his mouth.

"No, y'all not having them girls bother me for your numbers all day. I already have to avoid certain people since they saw y'all at that party," Lauren said.

Aunt Kathy laughed and said, "Speaking of women, there's this lady named Sharon Kelly calling here every day for you, Jerry."

Jerry remained quiet and continued eating.

"What happened? Cat got your tongue, Jerry?" Lauren asked, smirking.

"Don't laugh, David. My coworker won't stop asking me about you," Aunt Kathy said.

"You two better not bring any babies into this house," she quipped. She stopped laughing when Jerry asked her if she got through to Haiti.

"Listen, guys," was all she got to say before shots rang out.

Jerry grabbed Aunt Kathy, and I grabbed Lauren, and we dove on top of them for cover. Bullets hit the house, shattering windows, and glass was flying everywhere. It felt like an eternity before the shooting stopped. When it finally did, all we heard was a car speed off.

We all got up and checked to see that everyone was okay.

"What the hell was that?" Aunt Kathy cried out in horror.

No one said anything, and both Jerry and I were fuming.

We started to leave the kitchen when Aunt Kathy asked, "Where are you two going?"

"We're going to find the police!" I shouted, heading toward the door.

"I'm coming with y'all!" Lauren yelled.

"No you're not. Stay here and help Auntie clean up," Jerry ordered.

"Okay, but be careful," she said, and nodded.

"We'll be back."

We went straight to Gully's house.

"Yo, we have a change of plans," I said to him while I opened the door.

"What happened?" Gully asked, speaking in Creole.

"That nigga just shot my aunt's crib up!"

"Why? Does he know what's up?"

"Nah, it's something else we had a discussion about. I need you to go and pick up the car from Jimmy tomorrow morning."

"I just spoke to him, and he said that everything is ready," Gully responded.

"Good," I replied. We watched Jerry beat the shit out of Zoo.

"Yo, King, that's enough!"

"Nah, fuck this nigga and his whole family!" he screamed, still stomping on him.

I had to go and pull him off before he fucked around and killed Zoo. Before we even got the money.

"Piece of shit!" Jerry yelled in Creole, spitting on him. "Don't feed this nigga no more," Jerry said, and then left.

We all left, adrenaline pumping, knowing exactly what our next move would be.

25

103rd Precint

Detectives Lang and Kurtsky were at their desks, wrapping up a previous case, when a call came in about a shooting in Briarwood.

"Lang and Kurtsky," the captain said, "a call just came in about shots being fired in a residential area, and since Lorensky and Schmidt are out on a homicide case, y'all got next."

Lang and Kurtsky were not thrilled about having to leave the precinct in the middle of writing their reports. They knew this meant they would be pulling another overnighter.

"This shit is like a never-ending story, or should I say nightmare," Kurtsky said, grabbing his jacket from the back of the chair.

"Definitely a nightmare. Hopefully, this will be our last call before our shift is over, so we can process all this damn paperwork," Lang responded.

When they first arrived at the location, Lang saw at least forty shell casings in front of the house and shattered glass all over the steps. He immediately assumed somebody meant business, but after speaking to the owner of the house, he realized something was not adding up.

"So you mean to tell me nobody knows why your house became a target for a shooting that left more than forty casings in front of your house?" Lang inquired.

"No. We were having dinner in the kitchen when the shooting began," Aunt Kathy said, still shaken.

"Who are 'we'?" Lang asked.

"My daughter, my two sons, and myself," Aunt Kathy responded.

"Where are your sons now?"

"After the shooting, they said they were going to get the police," Aunt Kathy continued.

"When was that?" Detective Lang asked, taking notes.

"Almost an hour ago," she said, sounding unsure of herself.

"They left an hour ago and still have not returned or called?" Detective Lang quizzed.

"No."

"How old are your sons, ma'am?"

"Eighteen."

"What do they do?" Detective Lang asked.

"They go to school. Why are you asking all these questions about my sons?" she asked, becoming annoyed.

"Part of the investigation, ma'am." Detective Lang closed his note pad. "When your sons return, tell them to give me a call," he said, handing her his card.

"Okay."

"Have a nice evening," Detective Lang said, before leaving.

Aunt Kathy looked out through the shattered window as the two detectives drove off, and thought, *I don't know what's going on, but I hope the twins aren't involved. They left over an hour ago and still haven't returned home. I know they've been hanging around Lauren's boyfriend, and he's bad news, but now for this to happen! And to think I was about to tell them about what happened in Haiti.*

Lauren walked into the living room, only to find her mother staring out the window with tears falling from her eyes.

"It's going to be okay, Mom. Everything will work out," Lauren assured her.

"It's not only that, Lauren," she replied between sobs. "Everything seems to be going wrong. Something terrible has happened back home in Haiti."

"What happened, Mom?" Lauren asked, concerned at seeing her mother so shaken as she consoled her.

"I called and finally got through to a neighbor to check in on my sister, and I was told her house burned down, and we're not sure if anyone made it out alive."

"Oh my God! What? Did they find any bodies? How did this happen?" Lauren asked in astonishment.

"I don't know, sweetie. Part of the reason I wanted to sit down as a family was to let the boys know. I've been devastated ever since. I'm praying my sister is still alive and well. I can't allow myself to think otherwise. I just can't." She started to bawl.

"I don't even know what to say, Mom. I'm in shock," Lauren said, taking a seat on the couch.

Lauren led her mother to the couch and sat her down. Lauren placed her head on her mother's shoulder and closed her eyes.

First Zoo goes missing, our home gets attacked and now this. When will this nightmare end? she thought. *When?*

26

Jerry

David, Jinx, Gully, and I sat across the street in a car, watching Black and his crew set up for the drop-off. Black showed up with three other guys, and they were strapped. We gave him specific instructions about the drop-off, and he had already violated one. He was not alone.

"Them little niggas don't know who they're fucking with. I'll have to deal with them later. Right now, I have to worry about getting my little brother back," Black said before addressing his crew.

"I got a call last night telling me they wanted two million instead of the one million they originally requested. I had to pull a few strings, but I got it. They wanted me to drop the suitcase behind a bench in Goose Pond Park near Jamaica High School. I was told to wait under a tree, not too far from the money," Black explained.

"I wanted to arrive at least an hour before the drop-off so you guys could get into position. We were supposed to make the exchange at the same time, but I'm not stupid. That's why I had three of my best shooters along, just in case they wanted to act stupid. But once I get Zoo, it's on!"

"Yo, police coming!" one of the shooter's shouted while we were setting up.

Black turned and saw a black Impala with tints heading his way.

"Everybody be cool," he said.

The car door opened, and two plainclothes officers headed in his direction.

Both of them were black. One was tall and slim, and the other was short, with a normal build.

"What's going on, fellas? Just shooting the breeze?" the short one asked, with his hand on his holster.

"Listen, officer, we ain't done nothing wrong," Black said, showing the officer his hands.

"Whoa, keep your hands at your sides. Now I'm gonna need you guys to turn around and put y'all hands on the tree," the tall one commanded.

Black thought his voice sounded familiar, but he complied anyway. Black dealt with so many people there was no telling where he recognized this niggas voice from.

"Look what we got here on this one," the short one said, pulling a gun out of Black's waist band.

"Oh, shit. We must have hit the lottery because this one has a gun, too," the tall officer said.

"Don't I know you from somewhere?" Black asked the tall cop.

"Y'all were about to have some fun tonight, huh? Whoa, keep your hands on the tree," the tall officer warned, ignoring Black's question.

The cops took all their guns, pissing Black off because they no longer had any type of reinforcement.

"Turn around, all of you," the cops said.

When they turned, Black saw that the back passenger's side doors were open. A black garbage bag fell out, and two more cops exited the car. One of them picked up the garbage bag and walked toward Black and his crew.

"Son of a bitch," Black said, nervous and mad at the same time. Major was walking toward them, along with King who helped carry a bag.

"Here's your brother," Major said, tossing the bag in front of Black.

King pulled out a big-ass machete from his waist and said, "Yo, Jinx, go get the bag of money from behind the tree and put it in the truck."

"Go ahead and talk to your brother," King said, pointing to the bag.

Black watched them as he walked over to the bag. Before he even opened it, he could smell the metallic odor of blood. Black opened the bag and found Zoo's eyes staring into his. He turned around and threw up while at the same time, cursing.

"Yo, you thought you were going to get away with shooting my crib up!" Major screamed.

Jinx and Gully came back.

"Shoot them niggas over there!" King ordered, pointing at the other dudes who now looked like they wanted to run.

Jinx and Gully pointed the calico, and let 'em rip.

Black knew after hearing all those shots, he wasn't going to live. He looked down at the ground and said, "Fuck y'all niggas! I'm gonna see y'all bitch asses in hell!"

He looked up just in time to hear King say, "Have it your way." The last thing Black saw was the reflection of the streetlights on the edge of the machete as Jerry raised it above his head and lowered it in one swift motion, aiming for his head.

27

Jerry

After the payoff, we had to lay low for a while. The hood was talking about Black and his crew getting killed, and there was a lot of speculation, but no names had been called. I finally decided to call Mrs. Kelly back. She'd been blowing up my phone for the past couple of days. Since that little stunt she pulled, about not telling me that her husband was a cop, I'd been avoiding her. Besides that I had more important things to tend to, like Zoo and Black.

I was in a hotel with Mrs. Kelly, watching the news. I sparked up a blunt and glanced over at her. She'd been apologizing ever since I called her.

"I'm really sorry I didn't tell you my husband is a cop. It's just that I was so excited about you coming over it slipped my mind," she said, rubbing her hand over my chest.

"I don't think it would be beneficial for us if we keep seeing each other," I said, with my eyes glued to the tube.

She remained silent for a while, then asked, "What if I leave him?"

At first I thought she was nuts to consider leaving her husband for someone she barely knew. I certainly wasn't feeling her like that, but fuck it. It was her choice.

"Where would you go?" I asked.

"I don't know, but I've been saving my money for quite some time now. It should be enough to get a new place."

I thought about it for a second. Maybe it would be a good idea to have another spot to rest my head.

"If you're serious about this, then you're gonna have to leave everything behind," I said seriously.

"Okay," she said with finality.

"Alright, then I want you to leave everything except for a note telling him that you're leaving. Don't take anything. Start looking for a place immediately, preferably on Long Island."

"How are we going to keep up with the bills and all the other stuff?" she inquired.

"You let me worry about that," I said before stopping and turning up the volume on the TV.

"Jamaica High School is being closed for the week due to an ongoing police investigation. Officials say this is the most gruesome murder they have encountered in years. Police said, they received a call about shots being fired in Goose Ponds Park. Five bodies were found at the crime scene. One of the bodies was discovered in a garbage bag and was badly mutilated. The second was found headless, and the other three bodies were riddled with bullets. Over one hundred and fifty shell casings were found on the scene. Reporter John Smith, is at the location with an eye witness now," the reporter announced.

"Thank you, Jenna. We just received word that a clue was recovered from the scene that may give us further insight about these horrific executions. Police officials said there was a Haitian flag left on one of the bodies with a note attached to it. They didn't disclose what was written on the note, however, they did say these murderers referred to themselves as the Body Snatchers. I have a witness here who was allegedly at the scene at the time of these murders. Derek," John said, directing his attention to a slim-framed black man, wearing glasses.

"I was not there when the murders actually took place, but I did hear the shots being fired. I was walking my dog when all of a sudden I heard a hail of gunfire. Instinctively, I dropped to the ground behind a car and stayed down. After what felt like thirty minutes, I heard a car speed off. I finally got up once I heard police sirens."

"Thank you, sir. Live on the scene, this is John Smith. Back to you, Jenna."

"In other news, Governor Gary Long's son, James Long, has been reported missing. He is said to have disappeared two days ago, when he did not report to a club meeting," the anchorwoman reported.

A picture flashed across the screen, causing me to jump off the bed.

"Oh shit!" I yelled, looking at the TV. *That's the white boy I saw Block and Ricky take down to the basement,* I thought.

"More on that after this commercial break," Jenna said.

"What's wrong, baby?" Mrs. Kelly asked.

"Nothing. I'm gonna need you to get started on the move right away. I have to go home," I said, grabbing my gun and phone.

"How am I gonna get home?" she asked, sulking.

"I still have more time on the room, so you don't have to leave now," I said and handed her two hundred dollars along with a kiss. "Call me when you get home."

"I will," she said and laid back down.

And with that the wheels were set in motion.

Later on that evening...

As Mrs. Kelly left the hotel room, she looked back, giving a final check to the place. She looked at the bed with the sheets tossed all over, and a smile came across her face. *Umm, it was definitely a good night,* she thought. She went downstairs and saw a cab outside of the hotel waiting for her. Once she was inside, she thought about the different scenarios on how she could leave her husband.

It was almost midnight by the time Mrs. Kelly walked into her apartment. She wasn't expecting her husband to be home because he usually worked the late shifts on Thursdays.

He was sitting in the living room with an open bottle of whiskey on the coffee table and a shot glass held in his hand.

"Good morning, Sharon," he said to her as he raised the shot glass to his mouth.

"Hi, sweetie," Mrs. Kelly responded as she hung her bag on a hook in the closet.

"Where are you coming from at this time in the morning?" he asked.

"Oh, I was with Jasmine, and we went out for drinks after work," Mrs. Kelly responded quickly as she walked into the room.

"Really? And where exactly did y'all go?" he asked, taking another shot.

"A small lounge in the city," she replied.

"And, who did you let know you were going out with your friend Jasmine?" Jason asked, getting up from the table, following her into the room.

She began taking off her clothes, trying to avoid her husband. She just wanted to rush into the shower and wash away Jerry's scent. She washed up before leaving the hotel, but she normally took a shower when she arrived home, and if she didn't tonight, he would definitely think that she was up to no good.

"Don't you hear me talking to you, Sharon? Where are you?" Jason shouted.

"I'm in the shower, honey. I'll be right out!" she hollered from the bathroom.

Mrs. Kelly stepped out of the shower, only to find Jason waiting for her on the edge of the bed, still drinking his whiskey. "So like I said, who did you tell you were going out?" Jason asked, looking up at Mrs. Kelly with blood shot eyes.

"I didn't tell anyone because I didn't think I was child and had to report to anyone," Mrs. Kelly responded.

"Don't get smart with me now, Sharon. I know you just came from fucking another man, you fucking dirty bitch!" he slurred.

"What are you talking about, Jason? How long have you been out there doing you?" Mrs. Kelly said, putting on her night shirt.

"Who is he, Sharon? Someone told me they saw a guy leaving our apartment, and now, you coming home at damn near midnight," Jason said as he followed her around the room.

Mrs. Kelly didn't respond. Instead, she walked out of the room and into the kitchen to get something to drink.

"That's the shit I'm talking about. I'm talking to you, and you ignore me and walk away!" Jason shouted. He stormed into the kitchen after

Mrs. Kelly, grabbed her by the arm, and swung her around.

"What are you doing, Jason?" Mrs. Kelly shouted, shocked at his behavior.

In all the years they were married, Jason never laid a hand on her. She was frightened.

"I know you're cheating on me, Sharon! When was the last time we had sex?" Jason yelled, his hand still firmly gripped around her arm.

"I don't know what you're talking about. You're drunk, Jason," Mrs. Kelly said, trying to pull her arm free from Jason's tight grip.

Jason looked down and noticed a small red mark on her neck and became further enraged.

"Is that a hickey on your neck, Sharon? Did you just come from some man's house?" Jason yelled and hit her across the face. Mrs. Kelly held her face in total disbelief.

"Jason, you're hurting me. Please stop," she cried. "You're drunk. I just came out of the shower. The water was hot and I probably scrubbed too hard," she explained. "You're fucking crazy, Jason! I just came out of the shower!"

"You're lying, Sharon! You better tell me—or else!" he screamed, slapping her again and again in the face, causing her skin to bruise and swell.

"Get off me, Jason!" Mrs. Kelly protested, pulling away from him and running out of the room.

Jason ran after her and slammed the bedroom door behind him. He chased her around the bed before catching her and slamming her hard on to the bed.

"You think you can play me like that!" He huffed. He began un-buckling his belt. The smell of alcohol was seeping through his pores and smelled heavily on his breath.

Mrs. Kelly turned her face away as he spoke. She didn't respond and just closed her eyes, letting the tears roll down her face. Jason had managed to undo his pants and his dick was rock hard as he removed his boxers.

"Let's see who you've been fucking!" Jason roared, ripping off her shirt.

Mrs. Kelly tried fighting him off, but he just kept reminding her he was her husband. He pinned her arms down, spread her legs, and forcefully entered her. The pain was intense as Jason ripped through her walls. She was far from turned on, but that didn't stop him. The lack of moisture caused friction to burn her insides. Mrs. Kelly balled her fist and beat Jason with all her might, to no avail. Her reaction seemed to increase his excitement. Eventually she tired herself out and lay still as he continued to violate her. Silent tears wracked her body for what felt like an eternity.

Afterward, Mrs. Kelly went into the bathroom and locked the door. She took another hour long shower and cursed the day Jason was ever born. She walked out of the bathroom and found Jason passed out across the bed, snoring. *Selfish bastard,* she thought, and shot him an evil glare. She took her pillow into the living room to try to sleep away the pain. As she lay down on the couch, she continued plotting about a way to leave Jason. She knew he could use his resources at the police station to track her down, so leaving a note wouldn't be smart. Now she really needed a fail-proof escape plan because based on his behavior tonight if he found her, he'd without a doubt kill her.

28

Jerry

I rushed out of the hotel, thinking about what our next step should be. I took out my cell phone and called David.

"Yo, David, we have a problem. We have to meet with the fellas now!" I said with urgency.

"Yo, what happened?" David asked.

"I'll give you the rundown when I see you. For now, call the fellas and have them meet up at the spot, ASAP."

"Alright. Block is with me, and Gully should be here within the next fifteen minutes. I'll call Ricky. We'll meet you at the spot in like thirty minutes. One!"

We were all in attendance for the meeting. I couldn't help but be mad as I looked over at the white boy who was sleeping with his head covered.

"Tonight, I found out that the white boy we snatched is the governor's son. What the fuck is going on?" I shouted in Creole.

"I knew he had money, but I didn't know he was the governor's son," Block responded in Creole.

"Oh shit! Word!" Ricky said as he looked over at the kid.

"What the fuck? Gully said, astonished.

"No English," I said angrily in Creole. "While we're down here with him speak only Creole."

"See, that's why we told you to scope him out. You were supposed to gather all the information on him before you snatched him up," David said.

"Alright. Everyone calm down. It's too late for regrets or to start fighting about what should have been done. What we should worry about now is not making any more mistakes from here on out," Gully calmly stated in Creole.

"Did he see any of you?" David asked.

"Nah," Ricky said.

"You sure? What about the night y'all snatched him up?"

"Nah, man. We waited until he was about to get into his car, then grabbed him from behind, covering his head with a pillowcase. I'm sure he didn't see us."

"Good. Let's keep it that way because if he sees any of us, he can't leave here alive. Now, our plan must be bulletproof," I stated firmly.

"Alright, then, listen up," David said as he pulled a chair to the table.

We sat down and devised a plan on how we could get the ransom while keeping our identities safe and still manage to keep the governor's son alive. This was not going to be an easy task because now we had to worry about the FBI and the local police. Our plan had to be flawless, without any further mistakes.

One week later...

Jerry and I decided to stop by the house to check up on the guys and see how things were progressing with our plan on collecting the ransom money from the governor. As we walked into the basement, we noticed Jinx and Gully in the corner, hard at work with a blowtorch and electric saw, putting the final touches on the garbage bin we constructed for the job.

"How's everything coming along on your end?" I asked, looking at Gully and Jinx.

"It's a lot of work, but if you give us a few more days, everything should be finished," Jinx answered in Creole.

"You?" Jerry asked, looking at Ricky, Block, and Bones.

"Smooth. We just put together two more notes," Bones said, smiling.

"Good. Then everything will be set in motion in exactly one week.

I spoke to Gunz last night, and everything is good," I said, smiling.

"Haitians4Life," I said.

"Haitians4Life!" everyone replied.

29

FBI Headquarters

want your best men in your division working this damn case!"
Governor Long shouted into the phone, while trying to console
his wife. The governor woke up and found his wife in his son's room,
lying in his bed, crying. It was almost two weeks now, and the local
police still hadn't found any leads or clues about the kidnapping of his
son.

Now the FBI had taken control of the case. The bureau had sent
four agents out, and Agent Sean Camper was now appointed as the
lead agent in charge. Agent Camper had been in law enforcement since
the age of twenty-five. Growing up as a military brat, he idolized his
father and wanted to follow in his footsteps. Instead of joining the
military, he decided to enlist in law enforcement. He started working as
a local police officer, and within a couple of years, had moved up to the
Federal Bureau of Investigations. Since joining the Bureau, Camper
ran into a few snags as a result of his unorthodox methods. He was one
of those renegade agents, who always went against their supervisor's
orders, in order to catch their man. The director let him slide once in a
while because he was one of the best agents in his field. His first case
was a kidnapping and really hit close to home for Agent Camper. The
case lasted over a year, and the suspect had taken a special interest in
Agent Camper and also in his personal life. He threatened Agent Camper
and his wife and promised to kill everyone that Agent Camper ever
loved. Agent Camper finally caught his culprit, but it happened after it
broke apart his family and had taken a toll on him personally. He had to

take a brief leave of absence to regroup. Once he was able to pull it together he returned to work.

"Don't worry, Governor. We are the best in the division," Agent Camper said.

"While picking up the mail yesterday morning, Mrs. Long noticed a red-and-blue envelope. When she read the contents, she passed out. I spent thirty minutes, trying to stop her from going hysterical crying. The letters spelled out, "The Body Snatchers." I immediately phoned the FBI," Governor Long said.

"Is there anything else you can tell us about your son, sir?" Agent Camper asked, while taking notes. "Did he owe people money, or was he using drugs?"

"No, my son always had access to money, and no, he was not a drug addict. He is your typical teenager," he stated.

"Do you have any known enemies, or was there someone lately you may have offended?" Agent Camper asked.

"Not that I'm aware of. I haven't had any high-profile cases or new legislation to work on," Governor Long replied.

The governor walked over to the couch, sat down, and placed his head in his hands. Then, he looked up with anger in his eyes, and said, "What the fuck do they want with our son?"

"We have no idea at this point. The local police don't have any solid information on who these people are or their motives. All we know is they were involved in a murder out in Queens not long ago. My assumption is these guys will want a ransom. If that's indeed the case, then we'll be hearing from them again. The best thing to do is set up here, and the next time you hear from them, we'll be waiting," Agent Camper said.

"I don't care what it takes, I want my son back!" the governor exclaimed.

"We'll do everything we can, sir, to assure that your son is returned to you safely," Agent Camper replied.

As Agent Camper walked out with the agents, an image from his first case with the FBI flashed through his head. "I hope this is nothing like the first kidnapping I worked on," he said to himself.

30

Agent Camper

L isten, Camper. I'm getting shit from the higher offices right now. I don't give a damn about you not wanting a partner. Agent Joseph is a damn good agent, and he probably knows more about these punks than any of your guys. You better get acquainted—and fast," the director said, pointing his cigar at him. "Camper, you're still heading off the case, but if you fuck up, Joseph will take the lead. Capeesh? But before he gets here, let me give you a little background information on him," the director said, resting his cigar in the ashtray.

"Agent Joseph has been with the FBI for ten years, and he's part of the foreign counterintelligence team. He has worked on many high-profile cases like the Choloche Brothers and the kidnapping of the famous actress and philanthropist, Jadey Benton. Not to mention, the infamous Cuban drug lord, Sanchez Rodrigo. He helped foul the bombing of the senator's house and managed to have the perp inform us about another plot to assassinate the mayor of Boston. He is fluent in ten languages, including Creole, which is his native language. Besides the obvious, that's another reason why I want him working on the governor's son's kidnapping. He's from Haiti, and maybe he could give us some insight as to the motives of the Body Snatchers, so get accustomed to working with a partner," the director said as he picked up his cigar and took a pull.

Camper nodded and walked out of the director's office, then ran into Agent Joseph.

"What's going on?" Agent Joseph asked, extending his hand.

"Nothing much," Camper said, giving him a handshake. "So, you're Haitian, huh?" Camper asked as he walked toward the elevator.

"Everything about me," he said.

"So, do you know anything about the case yet?" Camper asked.

"Not really. I just know that the governor's son was kidnapped," Agent Joseph replied.

"Okay, so let me give you the rundown: About three weeks ago, Governor Long's son was reported missing. The last time the governor saw his son was that evening when he was preparing to go out. He was on his way to meet up with a group of friends. The next evening, when Junior didn't return home, the governor called the local police. About a week and a half ago, Governor Long received a red-and-blue ransom note from the Body Snatchers in the mail. At that time, we weren't even sure who the Body Snatchers were and how many of them there were, however, we believe they were involved in a local murder and a butchering in Jamaica, Queens. We also thought that they were Haitian because the ransom note along with the evidence left at the scene in Queens represents the Haitian flag," Camper explained before being interrupted.

"Agent Camper," another agent acknowledged, walking toward to them.

"Yeah?"

"The governor just called and said he received another note," she said.

"Ready?" Camper asked Agent Joseph.

"Readier than I've ever been," he replied.

31

Agent Camper

Agent Camper and Agent Joseph arrived at the governor's house the next day. During their ride together, Agent Camper got to know Agent Joseph a little better. Agent Camper was somewhat impressed with Agent Joseph's background, but still preferred working alone. Agent Camper also liked that everyone has positive things to say about Agent Joseph. The only thing people shared was that Agent Joseph was extremely protective of his native Haiti. He loved his country and would argue you to the death defending it.

Agent Camper and Agent Joseph arrived in Jamaica Estates, only to find the local police patrolling the area, and their team surveyed the governor's property. The governor was inside of his Queens home, talking on the phone and pacing the room. He wouldn't return to Albany until his son was back in his custody.

When Agent Camper walked into the house, he asked one of the agents where the governor was and was instructed that he was in his den.

When he walked into the governor's den, he asked, "Who received the letter? And by what method was it received?"

"Some kid brought it over," an agent replied.

"What kid?" Agent Camper asked, wearing a scowl.

"The kid lives up the block. He said he was riding his bike, when suddenly, a cab pulled up beside him. The back window rolled down, and someone called him. The person paid him fifty dollars just to bring this envelope to their house. He said he couldn't see the man's face because he had a hat, hoodie, and scarf covering his face," the agent responded.

"Shit," Agent Camper mumbled.

The note stated they want $20 million in unmarked hundred-dollar bills. The money is to be placed in five black garbage bags, which are to be placed into a Dumpster, behind Brooklyn's Stanley projects in East New York. There's no negotiating. Someone is to pick up the money, and once they check everything, the governor will receive another letter indicating his son's whereabouts. If they find anything wrong with the money, or if their man never makes it, the governor can expect to find his son placed in a body bag, chopped in pieces. Another letter will follow with the day to drop the money off. The letter ended with their alias, The Body Snatchers."

"Listen, Agent Camper, I don't want any gimmicks or stunts being pulled. This is my son we're talking about, and I want him returned to me, safe and sound. They said we have three days to get the money. I want the money dropped off, and I want my son back! Do you hear me?" he yelled, looking Agent Camper straight in the eyes.

"I understand that, but let us be the FBI. You called on us to help. We're the best in this field for a reason. We'll get your son back, governor, so stop demanding and start understanding," Agent Camper insisted, maintaining eye contact.

"Listen to me, you piece of shit! If anything—and I mean anything—happens to my son, I'll have you out looking for a job on the moon, so you better understand who it is you're talking to!" the governor contested at the top of his lungs.

Agent Camper turned his back to the governor and walked out.

Walking back to the FBI trailer that was parked out front, Agent Camper spotted Agent Joseph talking to the kid who had delivered the letter to the governor. Agents were moving throughout the house, setting up wire taps and video surveillance cameras. The scene in the governor's house reminder Agent Camper of his first case at the bureau. It was the case that almost took him down. Freddy Elmer was the name of the low-down, dirty sick bastard. He deserved whatever he got, and Agent Camper only wished the case would've come to a close sooner. It practically destroyed his life. Especially after Freddy Elmer violated Agent Camper's personal space and tried to kidnap his ex-wife. She left Agent Camper because she wasn't able to handle the stress that came with being married to someone in law enforcement, not to mention her near-death incident, and the emotional toll became too much for her. Agent Camper did not want this case to be prolonged. He wanted to apprehend the suspects and make them tell the location of where the governor's son was being held.

Walking into the trailer, he spoke to the team, "Okay, fellas, let's set the wheels in motion." His team looked up with eagerness in their eyes, ready to work.

The men remained stationed at the governor's house for six days and in that time never received a letter. They had a man stationed at the local post office just in case the Body Snatchers decided to use their facility to drop off the letter. They also had agents surveying all the mailboxes within a thirty-mile radius of the governor's house, looking for any suspicious individual. All packages coming into the governor's house were thoroughly inspected. There was an outpouring of sympathy from friends and colleagues, and the governor was receiving a lot of flowers and cards from friends expressing their sorrow, but there was still no letter from the Body Snatchers.

Finally, they got a break, and it was only due to the keen eye of Agent Joseph who was doing his daily check of the deliveries and noticed something out of the ordinary with one of the bouquets of flowers. The vase held six blue roses, six red roses and one white. He never saw blue roses before, so he walked over for inspection. He decided to pick up the vase and look for the sender. Surprisingly, there wasn't one. Agent Joseph looked beneath the vase and noticed a red piece of paper attached to the bottom. His eyes opened wide as he realized this was the last clue they were waiting for. Immediately, he rushed out of the room and into the office where Agent Camper was sitting.

"Agent Camper, I think this is what we were looking for!" Agent Joseph said, handing him the note from under the vase.

"Holy shit! When did this come in?" Agent Camper asked.

"This morning, along with the other deliveries. I was looking for anything out of the ordinary and noticed the blue roses."

"Good job, Agent Joseph," Agent Camper said, opening the note.

Okay, this was what we were waiting for. Tomorrow we'll take this show on the road."

32

Agent Camper

Agent Camper read the note, confirming the time and location of the drop-off, and called the staff for an emergency meeting.

"Okay, fellas, we've got what we were waiting for. The drop-off location is in Brooklyn," he stated.

"Where in Brooklyn?" an agent asked.

"East New York. I'm going to need at least ten agents doing surveillance of the area. Here is the address, Team A will head out within the next fifteen minutes to this location and set up. Keep me posted if you see anything out of the ordinary. Keep your earpiece on and stay out of sight. That will be our form of communication," Agent Camper directed.

"Agent Joseph will head Team B, and they will have the money. Agent Joseph, you should get the money from the governor's assistant, and make sure it's in the denominations they requested."

"Okay, I'm on it," Agent Joseph said, leaving the room.

"We should head out there at least four hours before the designated time. Agent Brown, I need you to gather all the equipment we may need for this mission. Agent Shaw, I need you to be in charge of communications. Make sure all the earpieces and walkie-talkies are working. We cannot afford any mistakes with this dropoff. I need all t's crossed and all i's dotted. We cannot drop the ball on this one, guys," Agent Camper said, adamantly.

"I'm going to speak to the governor and let him know of the new developments. By the time I get back, we should be ready to head out and get the governor's son back to his sheltered and lavish life," Agent Camper said, walking out of the office.

When they arrived at the location, there were about ten agents in the perimeter, including the agents who were responsible for dumping the money into the Dumpster, located in the back of a building behind the projects in East New York, Brooklyn. Across the street, it was really busy with pedestrian traffic, due to the stores and a Laundromat. Agents Joseph and Camper were in the van, waiting for the pickup so they could make their next move. Agent Camper glanced at his watch and saw that it was the appointed time to make the drop.

"Okay, let it rip!" Agent Camper yelled, through his earpiece.

An agent hopped out of a van that was parked nearby and went to open the back door. There were five bags there, but only three were filled with money, leaving the kidnappers with only ten million dollars as opposed to the twenty that they requested. The other two were filled with newspapers. There was no way Agent Camper was going to allow those hoodlums to get away with this. Not under his watch. Once he got the pickup guy, he knew he would surely make him talk. The agent dropped the bags and walked back to the van.

"We're set," he said.

Now, the only thing to do was to wait for them.

Four hours later...

"Hey, chief, you think this is the right one?" Agent Camper asked through the headset.

"Yeah, I'm sure. They're probably playing some type of game with us. Let's keep it cool and keep our eyes open."

Two hours later...

The streetlights were on, and some of the stores were beginning to close. Agent Joseph and Agent Camper noticed someone moving toward the Dumpster holding a garbage bag in his hand.

"Okay, fellas, get ready," Agent Camper said, finally excited.

But the guy just opened the lid and threw the bag in, and then walked away.

"Hey, chief, did you hear that?" Agent Joseph asked.

Agent Camper heard, but didn't answer. He hopped out of the van and ran toward the Dumpster. "It's not possible," he mumbled to himself with each long stride. "It's just not possible." Flipping the lid he looked inside in horror, and then he dropped to his knees and said, "Fuck, Fuck, Fuck!"

There was only one bag in the Dumpster. The bags with the money were gone.

33

Agent Camper

The receptionist greeted Agent Camper when he walked into the director's office. "Agent Camper, they're waiting for you."

He entered the director's office and saw the governor seated in the chair by the far right window. Agent Joseph was sitting about ten feet away from him. Agent Camper shut the door and sat in the chair opposite Agent Joseph.

"Read this," the director said, sliding an envelope toward Agent Camper.

He already knew who it was from. He opened the red-and-blue envelope and began reading the letter.

THIS IS THE LAST LETTER YOU CAN EXPECT FROM US. YOU HAVE BEEN WARNED IN THE PREVIOUS LETTER NOT TO MISTAKE US AS A JOKE. YOU HAVE GRAVELY DISAPPOINTED US. YOU HAVE BREACHED OUR CONTRACT. WE ARE IN RECEIPT OF TEN MILLION. WE REQUESTED TWENTY. IN RETURN, YOU WILL PAY DEARLY FOR YOUR LACK OF RESPECT. YOU WILL NOT GET YOUR SON BACK IN ONE PIECE. YOUR INSULT WAS DETRIMENTAL. YOU WILL RECEIVE A CALL REGARDING WHERE YOUR SON'S BODY PARTS ARE LOCATED. THANK YOU FOR YOUR COOPERATION.

—THE BODY SNATCHERS

Agent Camper's body was burning up with rage. These were some arrogant bastards! Throughout his career, Agent Camper arrested at least one hundred convicts, but never had been made to look and feel like a fool. This was far from over, he thought. It wasn't over yet!

"You better start talking," the director said to Agent Camper while lighting a cigar.

Agent Camper explained everything to the director and the governor, from the very beginning. He paused when the time came to explain the disappearance of the money.

"Apparently, the back of the Dumpster had a small opening in the rear. The Dumpster was connected to the building wall. When we were finally able to pull the Dumpster away from the wall, we noticed the hole. The hole led to the building's basement, which had a passage leading to an exit. The buildings are all connected and ended a few blocks over. That was how the culprits made their getaway, sir," Agent Camper explained.

"You've disgraced this department and disappointed me," the director said, shaking his head.

"I want this motherfucker's badge!" Governor Long shouted as he jumped to attack Agent Camper "Governor, I'm sorry for what happened. Please understand what I did was normal procedure. The culprits that got away were out of my control," Agent Camper said, pleading his case.

The governor walked over and punched him squarely in the face.

"Governor!" the director uttered, jumping out of his seat.

"Your job will be the last thing I'd want if my son isn't returned in one piece," Governor Long said, slamming the door as he walked out.

"This is Agent Joseph's case now, so hand over the files to him," the director said with disgust.

"Chief, I know I can handle this case. I just need enough time to run an investigation," Agent Camper said, rubbing his face.

"Clear out your desk, and don't forget to leave your gun and badge before you leave this office," he said, as he returned to his desk. Agent Camper placed his gun and badge on the desk and left with only one thing on his mind: revenge.

34

Haiti

Chico had not been handling the death of his son Mario well. He had turned into a monster and became one of the most ruthless and heartless criminal businessman in Haiti. He always had a bad temper, but now it was totally out of control. His actions were callous, heartless, and brutal. He even lost pride in his appearance, and that was one thing Chico was big on—his looks. He used to tell Mario the first impression was everything, and it could either make or break a deal. Now, he was seen around town, wearing week-old outfits, dingy clothes, and had an unshaven face. His close friends and business partners noticed the change in his behavior and warned him the change in his attitude could lead to his demise. They understood he was going through a painful loss, especially after losing his only son, but business still had to be carried out professionally. He had invested all of his resources and attention into finding the locations of Jerry and David.

On previous occasions Chico would take it easy on people who borrowed money. Especially if it was small amounts, but now if you didn't have his money within one week of the due date, you were in trouble. He would have his goons come and pay you a visit and either break body parts or beat you to the point beyond recognition. He was angry that the twins stole his money and now he was taking his anger out on everyone else. Consequently, he went looking in his log book for people who had outstanding balances with him and personally went to collect them.

While searching, he ran across a woman by the name of Rose who owed him $3,500 from two years ago. Chico made a note in his book that she promised to pay him back by November of last year. Chico hadn't received a dime since then—not even a phone call from her—so he decided to have his goons visit her neighborhood in order to find her whereabouts. After some painful persuasion from his guards, her cousin finally relented. He told them she had moved to the States. However, she was expected to be back within a couple of days to visit a sick family member. The goons then took whatever valuables they could find before brutally beating him and leaving him badly injured right in the middle of the street.

Rose arrived in Haiti at her cousin's house two days after the incident, and Chico's goons were right there waiting for her. They captured her and brought her to one of Chico's hideout spots. She tried to resist at first, and after being knocked around by the guards for a while, she finally complied.

"Sak Pase, Rose, sweetie," Chico said. "Long time no see, huh?"

"Sak Pase," Rose said.

"How is life in the States? Beautiful place, don't you agree?" Chico asked sarcastically.

Rose didn't respond.

"What happened to my $3,500 that was supposed to be paid to me last year?"

"I got into a little trouble and had to leave the country, but I intended to send the money to you once I got on my feet, Chico," Rose pleaded, stuttering with fear.

"So when were you planning on letting me know that you left Haiti?" Chico asked, getting upset.

"I'm sorry, Chico. I—" was all Rose was able to say before Chico slapped her across the face, causing her bottom lip to split open and bleed.

Rose continued to plead with Chico for her life. She even offered to work off her debt. His guards laughed at the suggestion and pushed her to the ground. Chico walked over to Rose and asked, "So, do you have my money today?"

Rose had nine hundred dollars in her bank account and had planned on using it to help her great-aunt who was in medical need.

"Chico, please spare me! I don't have the money right now, but I'll try to get you something by the end of the day. I have a son and husband who need me!" Rose begged with teary eyes and a bloody lip.

Chico tensed and the look in his eyes was now cold and dark. He lowered his head in order to stare Rose directly into her eyes, while he slid his hands around her neck and said, "Son? Son? My son was killed and taken away from me! So, don't tell me anything about your son because I have no family now!"

Chico loosened his grip around Rose's neck and pushed her down on the ground. He walked out of the barn, furious she would have had the nerve to even mention her family to him. He gave the signal to his guards to finish the job and kill her.

Walking out to his car, Chico received a phone call. He didn't recognize the number and was going to let it go to voicemail, but then decided to answer.

"This is Chico," he responded, feeling irritated.

After five minutes of listening to what the caller had to say, Chico responded, "Are you positive? Okay, if this doesn't follow through, I will personally kill you!" Chico hung up the phone.

Chico was quiet for the entire ride back home. In the back of his mind, he hoped the caller had given him the correct information. He pulled his phone out of his blazer pocket and made a phone call. He informed the person on the other line to have his private jet fueled and ready because he would need it soon.

Fifi and Sophie were on their way to Fifi's house. They were coming back from a long day of shopping at the local boutiques. Sophie was tired of seeing Fifi moping around her house, eating everything in sight, and looking depressed. She figured a day of shopping would definitely do the trick.

"Thank you for always being there for me, Sophie. I know I've been a drag to hang out with lately," Fifi said.

"No problem, girl. I just know I was tired of seeing you look like the world was coming to an end. It was either this or strangling you," Sophie said, imitating choking Fifi.

They both laughed at the joke, knowing it was half true because Fifi had been in such a funk since the death of her cousin and since David disappeared.

"I've been thinking a lot lately, about the night of Mario's death, and I have to tell you something," Fifi said, looking down at the ground.

"The weirdest thing happened that night. After we had sex, I heard a noise in the house then out of nowhere David punched me in the face, and he never hit me before," Fifi said before being interrupted by Sophie.

"He did what to you? Did he lose his fucking mind that night?" Sophie asked with her hand on her hip.

"That's the thing, I don't think it was David that hit me. After watching the tape over and over, I noticed something. The tape showed Jerry entering the house a couple of minutes after us. But it wasn't Jerry, it was David. I could tell because I gave David a gold bracelet for our two-month anniversary, and he was wearing it that night. But, that's not all," Fifi said, stopping to look at Sophie face-to-face.

"I'm not sure if you noticed that I gained weight or have been eating more lately," Fifi said.

"I did notice the increase in your appetite, but I thought it was from your being depressed," Sophie responded.

"I'm pregnant, and I'm positive that Jerry is the father."

Sophie stared at Fifi in astonishment with her mouth wide opened and shouted, "Oh, oh!"

You're what, and who is the father?"

Sophie instinctively put her hands onto Fifi's stomach and felt the firmness of her belly. Fifi always wore baggy clothes, and because she was petite and was carrying small, it helped conceal her pregnancy from family and friends.

"When are you due?"

"This month, but I haven't told my uncle yet because I know he's going to freak out. He's been so preoccupied with his vendetta that we haven't really had a chance to talk, but I know I have to do it soon. Ever since Mario died, he barely even acknowledges me. On most occasions he walks right past me, and when he does look my way his eyes are filled with so much hatred. If he ever found out who the father is, he would completely disown me," Fifi said. Her eyes were filled with sadness. "I'll tell him and I'll just say I don't know who the father is."

"That sounds like the best thing to do because what are you going to tell him once he hears a crying baby in the house?" Sophie exclaimed.

The girls finally reached Fifi's house and decided to get something to eat. The maid was in the kitchen cooking rice and red beans, oxtails, and a side of macaroni salad. They decided to fix a plate and sit in Fifi's room, and continue their conversation. Fifi explained to Sophie how relieved she felt, finally being able to tell someone about what was going on. Fifi decided to speak to her uncle later on during the night when he got home.

Later that evening, Sophie and Fifi waited outside for Sophie's aunt to pick her up. While waiting, Sophie noticed movements in the shed next to the driveway. She focused her attention on the shed, trying to see what or who was inside. Fifi was distracted by one of the maids who was asking her a question and didn't notice Sophie was walking over to the shed. She opened the door and that was when Fifi called her and asked her where she was going. By this time, whoever was in the shed was now staring at Sophie.

"Who is this little girl, Fifi?" Sophie asked, looking confused.

"Oh that was the other thing I wanted to tell you. You heard what happened to David's family, right?"

"Yeah, I heard. That was terrible," Sophie responded.

"Well, the night when the incident occurred, I returned to the twins' house and found their sister hiding behind a pile of charcoal. She was traumatized after hearing what happened to her family. She snuck out of the house through the window while her mother and brother were being tortured. I took her in, and she's been staying in the shed ever since then. I tried my best to make it as comfortable as possible for her."

Sophie had a look of amazement on her face. Before she could respond, her aunt arrived. She blew the horn over and over bringing unwanted attention to Fifi's home, so she scurried off toward the car. Sophie jumped into the car and promised to call later to continue their conversation.

Fifi was simply relieved to finally share her burden with someone else. Now all she had to do was talk to her uncle Chico and figure out what to do next about Loria.

35

Detective Lang

etective Lang couldn't get the Briarwood shootout off his mind. It just didn't make sense that a quiet residential neighborhood that never had a history of crime would now have a shootout. Since he never received a call from the twins about the incident, he decided to stop by their house to pay them a visit. The twins' demeanor was calm, and they answered the few questions he asked, but something just didn't sit right with Detective Lang. Maybe it was a policeman's intuition, but he left the house having more questions than with which he came, so he decided to open up a case file on the twins, unknown to his partner and superiors.

He had been following them for a few weeks now, and they appeared to behave like your average teenagers—they went to school, hung out, and then went directly home. He didn't see anything out of the ordinary so far.

Detective Lang tried to figure out a way to tell them apart, and was finally able to by a stroke of luck.

Detective Lang discovered they went by the aliases King and Major. No one could really tell the difference between them either, except that Jerry drove the blue BMW and David drove the green one. They were Haitian and recently enrolled in a GED school and seemed to be very popular among the students. Jerry allegedly was the sneaky, wild one, while David appeared to be the quiet, calm one. They had a team of friends who apparently held the same status. After a background check on their friends, Detective Lang found out all of them had served time in juvenile detention centers with the exception of Jerry and David. They seemed to have a reputation on the streets and among their peers. All of these guys wore expensive clothing and drove luxury cars, but only a few of them held jobs. After school, they hung out at a house on Highland and didn't leave until the wee hours of the morning. After more digging into their backgrounds, he found out the entire crew was Haitian. Something suspicious was definitely going on with these guys. Detective Lang figured whatever they were doing was probably illegal, but they were extremely clever and seemed to be covering their tracks well.

As Detective Lang continued with his investigation, he noticed one of the twins was always in the company of one of their teachers. At first, it didn't seem unusual because he only observed them interacting around school property. Until one day, when he saw Jerry and the teacher walking into a hotel together. He realized which twin it was because Jerry drove the blue car. *Students and teachers sleeping together is not that far-fetched nowadays,* Detective Lang thought. He waited for them to exit the hotel, then went in and asked the clerk for information about Mrs. Kelly and proceeded to perform a background check on her.

Weeks went by, and Detective Lang became more familiar with the twins' patterns. They were very close and spent a great deal of time together as well as with their friends. They had many acquaintances that he thought were kind of strange, especially since they were only in high school. He watched them meet with Kim Lewis, a successful business mogul, and Nancey Rose, the owner of one of the largest publishing firms on the East Coast and wondered what they had in common.

During one of Detective Lang's surveillances, he thought he was spotted and that the investigation was over. He followed the twins to a meeting area outside of the city and watched as they got out the car to meet with a big stocky guy who looked like a bouncer. While he was sitting in the car watching the guys exchange words, Detective Lang accidentally hit the headlights and caught the attention of Jerry, David, and their acquaintances. They all stopped what they were doing and looked toward the direction of the car. Detective Lang cursed himself for hitting the switch and quickly put his car in gear, then drove off. He figured this was the only option he had to not let on that he was following them. As he drove off, he glanced into his rearview mirror and wondered what they were meeting about and who that big guy was. He couldn't get answers today, but he was sure he was on to something.

36

Brooklyn

It had been ten days since the twins arranged the exchange with the governor, and they had reneged on the deal. The Body Snatchers didn't want it to end this way, and if they didn't do what they had promised, the authorities wouldn't take them seriously the next time they struck. Now, the governor's son's death would be yet another example of what the Body Snatchers were capable of doing. Ricky and Block were supposed to handle the final rights of Mr. Long, then make the drop-off.

They decided to contact the local news station, JBCJ, where the sexy news anchorwoman Jenna Hillman worked to give them the first dibs on the breaking news. Once the drop was made in Brooklyn, Block was to call the news station and speak directly to Jenna Hillman. At precisely 8:30 P.M., Block made the call to the news station and informed Jenna Hillman about the drop-off. After the call, Block and Ricky made their way back to Brooklyn.

An hour later, Block and Ricky saw a car pull up at the corner of Nostrand Avenue and President Street. They watched as Jenna Hillman walked out of the car and approached the Dumpster, attempting to open it.

"Yo, Major, I made the call, and everything is in motion. We're waiting to see what happens next," Block said, talking into the walkie-talkie and speaking in Creole.

"Hey, excuse me. Can you help me open this Dumpster, please?"

Jenna Hillman asked a homeless man and pulled twenty dollars out of her coat pocket to pay him.

He looked at the money, then looked back at her for a second in total disbelief.

"That's just to open the lid?" he asked in a raspy voice, looking around him.

"Yes."

After a few minutes of struggling with the lid, the homeless man finally opened it. Jenna leaned forward and found two black garbage bags.

"I knew it!" she said, pissed.

"Can I get my money, lady?"

"Yeah."

She handed him the money, and suddenly, something caught her attention. "Oh, and one more thing: Can you grab that bag for me?" she asked, pointing to the bag that had a red-and-blue cloth tied around the neck.

Jenna stood motionless staring at the bag.

"Come on, lady, you just have to open the damn thing," he complained.

Jenna took another twenty from her wallet, and handed it to him. He struggled to pull the bag out and dropped it hard on the ground.

"Damn, that shit's heavy," he said.

She went to tear open the bag open, but the smell made her move back.

"What you afraid of, garbage?" he asked.

He opened the bag and stared at the contents for a few second before yelling and passing out.

Jenna Hillman leaned over, looking into the bag, and ran to her car to call the news station and police.

37

Detective Lang

Detective Lang had been keeping a close surveillance on the twins and their friends for the past month. His primary focus had been on the twins, but lately, Ricky and Block had moved up on his radar. They seemed to be inseparable and always looked like they were up to something. Two days ago, he watched Ricky and Block walk into a house on Highland Avenue carrying an industrial-sized saw, a blow-torch, and several other items he couldn't identify. Their movements were becoming more and more suspicious to Detective Lang.

Later that evening, Detective Lang watched Ricky and Block re-move a large garbage bag from the house on Highland Avenue. The garbage bag had a red-and-blue cloth tied around the neck. They placed the bag into the trunk of a Chevy Impala that looked identical to the one Detective Lang was driving and got into the car and drove off.

He decided to follow them to see where they were taking the sus-picious looking bag.

Detective Lang trailed them until they reached a Dumpster in Brook-lyn. They got out of the car and threw the bag into the Dumpster, then got into their car and sat there, waiting.

Three hours later, a Caucasian woman who looked very familiar to him pulled up next to the Dumpster and got out of her car. She looked around first and spoke to a black homeless man. He opened the lid to the Dumpster and struggled, trying to pull out the same bag he saw the guys loading into their car trunk earlier. The man then proceeded to tear the bag open, screamed then fell to the ground. Suddenly, their car took off. The woman ran back to her car and proceeded to make a call.

Detective Lang opened his car door and ran toward the bag. He saw the red-and-blue cloth and realized it was the Haitian flag—the same one used in the Goose Ponds murder. He opened the bag and turned around and grimaced. He then took out his phone and dialed the number from the business card he had received from the Feds.

"Quantico," the telephone operator said.

"This is Detective Lang. I want to speak to Agent Joseph," he said.

"In regards to?" she asked.

"This is fucking urgent! Get me Agent Joseph—now!" Detective Lang yelled.

"Just a second," she said.

A moment later, he came on.

"Agent Joseph," he said, sounding a bit irritated.

"This is Detective Lang from the 103rd precinct. I just witnessed two perps drop a bag with a body inside of it. I suspect these guys are part of the organization your boys have been looking for," Detective Lang said, trying to remain calm.

"You're not talking about those Body Snatchers bandits, are you?" asked Agent Joseph, now sounding much more interested.

"I believe so, sir," Detective Lang said, looking at the Haitian flag tied around the neck of the bag.

"Listen, I'm sending down some ag—" he said before Detective Lang cut him off.

"With all due respect, I'm going to arrest these suspects and bring them in. I believe there are five more. I know a set of twins played a major role in this operation. I have nothing solid yet, but I believe they are the leaders. However, tonight I'm going to pick up the guys I saw at the scene, and hopefully get some information out of them," Detective Lang said, staring at the woman in front of him, finally recognizing her.

"Detective. you better listen, and listen clear, hotshot! Stand down now. If you think that for one second I'm going to let you sabotage this investigation, then you got another thing coming. If you go against my orders, then I'm going to have your badge floating in the Hudson River along with the sewage. Got me?" Agent Joseph said, hanging up.

38

Jerry

I couldn't stop shaking my head at this nonsense. I was in our room watching David pack for his trip to Miami with Britney tomorrow. He was going to meet up with the connect, since Black and Zoo were officially out of the picture.

"I can't believe you. Out of all the women chasing you, you're going to take Britney to Florida with you?" I said, chuckling.

"So. What about you? Mr. Love 'em and leave 'em!

"You got jokes, huh?"

Suddenly, I heard the basement door to our room open.

"Hey, guys," Lauren said, coming down the steps.

"What's up?" I said, puffing on a blunt.

"Where do you think you're going?" she asked David and sat down on his bed.

"None of your business, nosey," he said as he sat down beside her.

"Mmm, don't think I don't know what's going on. That girl has been running her mouth all week. I'm going to Miami this week with David," she said, imitating Britney.

"Ha ha, that's how she sounds too," I said, laughing.

"I don't know why you're laughing, Jerry. Kara won't stop crying and asking me why you don't call her. Y'all are dogs. You screw her, then don't even call her," she said, shaking her head.

"Nah, it's not even like that. She knows I got love for her. As a matter of fact, I'm gonna call her tonight," I said, passing the blunt to David.

"How you been holding up, anyway?" David asked.

"I've been alright. I miss Zoo a lot. I mean, I knew he was a dog, but I loved him, you know? Our relationship was kind of rocky, but who knows what could have happened?" she said, taking the blunt from David before continuing.

"I knew whatever he was into wasn't necessarily good, but I never thought his life would end so soon. He used to talk about leaving the game, but he didn't know how Black would feel about it. He loved Black to death, but I guess all that's changed now. That's fucked up, what they did." Tears began to stream down her face.

"Yeah," I said.

"When I go to school now, all they talk about is what the Body Snatchers did to those guys in the park, and it must have been true that the Haitians who did it chopped up the bodies." She paused. "But I'm just going to take this relationship shit slowly. This is just too much for me." She wiped the tears from her face.

"That's a good idea," I said, pulling two thousand dollars out of my pocket. "Here, go get something nice for yourself. You're going to need to start having fun, and don't let that shit get to you. You deserve better than that nigga, anyway," I said, picking the dirt from my nails.

"Yeah, there are better men out there for you, besides drug dealers, you know? I'm sure there are some decent dudes at your school, but we've got to approve of them first 'cause some of them look kind of fruity," David joked.

"You better watch Britney while you're out there. She might just trap you the way she be talking about you," She giggled.

It was an innocent night with the three of us laughing, cracking jokes, and smoking. I'd look back at this night and wish life were always just this simple.

39

Jerry

David's been gone for two days now. It felt kind of funny being alone, especially after all the shit we went through. I don't know what I'm going to do tonight. I was fucked up already from drinking and smoking for the past two hours. I felt as though the TV was watching me. I was on my bed watching that cute-assed white girl on JBCJ News. I turned up the volume to hear what she was saying.

"The Body Snatchers are at it again, and this time, it's the governor's son. The body that was found in the Dumpster earlier this week has now been confirmed to be James Long, the son of Governor Gary Long. The governor was not available for comment. James Long's body was mutilated and placed in a black garbage bag, and the medical examiners were unable to identify the body until recently, due to the body's condition. Neither the FBI nor the local authorities have any leads on the alleged killers. Community members are now starting to feel unsafe in their homes."

A cute black girl suddenly appeared on the screen.

"It's sad, you know, because I'm Haitian, and I don't want people thinking we are some kind of terrorists or thugs," she said.

"Sak pase!" I yelled, high as hell.

"Neg' La!" a voice behind me said.

I jumped off the bed to see who it was. My vision was kind of blurry, but as it started to clear, I saw a big black dude and four other guys holding guns and pointing at me.

"You didn't think I would find you, huh?" he said in Creole.

"How did you get in here?" I yelled, angrily.

"Is that the welcome I get after all this time? I brought you a little gift." He smiled and threw an envelope down onto the bed.

"Fuck you, Chico!" I spat.

He laughed and said, "Go ahead. Open it."

I looked at his goons dressed all in black grilling me with the most contemptuous look. I reached for the envelope and opened it. When I saw what was inside, I fell to my knees, and I began to cry.

"You dirty motherfucker!" I yelled.

With that, Chico kicked me in the jaw and proceeded to knock me out.

40

Aunt Kathy

Aunt Kathy was in the dining room cleaning and thinking about how her home had been violated only weeks ago. Since then she had become extremely paranoid. That night was the scariest of her life. The holes in her walls remained as evidence of the violence done to her home. Her expensive artwork from Paris was now ruined among other valuables.

Aunt Kathy never cared for Lauren's boyfriend, Zoo. She found him to be rude and extremely disrespectful. He often strolled into her home wearing his pants hanging off his backside without acknowledging her. After many repeated incidents, she told Lauren he was no longer welcome in their home. And though she didn't like him for her daughter, she felt bad when Lauren told her about his untimely demise. Regardless of her personal feelings, she'd never wish death on him.

She no longer had to worry about Zoo, but her twin nephews were another story altogether. Aunt Kathy had a strong feeling they were up to no good. They thought she was oblivious to their wardrobe makeover, which she knew wasn't cheap. To top that off, one of her neighbors mentioned seeing one of the twins driving a BMW, and she noticed at one point how friendly the twins were with Zoo. That is what initially set her radar off, so she had a strong feeling they too were involved in drugs. Lauren never told her that drug dealing was Zoo's occupation, but she was no fool. Zoo didn't have an education that she knew of; he drove a Range Rover and wore more gold than Mr. T did when he starred in the A-Team. The twins told her they had a part-time job, but unless they hit Lotto or were the new owners of Def Jam records, she knew they were lying. Unfortunately, she had been too busy to address the situation, but she was going to have a talk with them—and soon. It was long overdue. Not to mention the fact that she still hadn't broken the news about their mother. She was hoping to learn more about the situation, but she wasn't making much progress and now she was seriously concerned. It wasn't like her sister to not get in touch with her. She was really worried now. Every time she attempted to tell the twins that her sister's house burned down, something came up. It was either she was working double shifts or the twins simply were never home. Their schedules never seemed to match. They really needed to sit down as a family.

The chime of the doorbell took her out her reverie. When she looked through the peephole, she saw a familiar face, but wasn't sure where she knew the woman from.

"Yes, how may I help you?" Aunt Kathy asked.

"Hi, Ms. Benton. It's Mrs. Kelly. I'm Jerry's teacher. I was wondering if I could speak with you for a moment," she said with worry in her voice.

Aunt Kathy quickly opened the door for Mrs. Kelly.

"Hi, Ms. Benton. I was wondering if Jerry is home," she said nervously as she ran her hand through her hair. "You and I met during the orientation when Jerry and David first started."

"Yes, yes. I remember now. Well, I'm not sure if either of them is home, but I'll double check. Is there some kind of problem?" Aunt Kathy asked. She found it rather unusual this woman would appear at her doorstep looking for her nephew. Aunt Kathy gave Mrs. Kelly a once-over as she stood before her. This woman was a few years shy of her age. Aunt Kathy sincerely hoped there was nothing going on with her eighteen-year-old nephew and this woman who claimed to be married. She was undeniably beautiful, but she was still a grown woman.

"No, it's just that he hasn't been to school over the past few days, and I was wondering if everything was alright. Jerry's a very good student, and I would hate for him to fail, especially now, since he's so close to graduating," Mrs. Kelly replied.

"Yes, that would be a shame," Aunt Kathy said, unconvinced that was the only reason for this out-of-the-blue visit. "Come inside and let me see if he's home." Aunt Kathy guided her into the living room to have a seat, then she went downstairs into the basement to the boys' room. She was scared of what she might find, especially since she hadn't been down there to clean in over a month. Sneakers, shoe boxes, hangers, and clothes were strewn all over the place. The beds were unmade, ashtrays were overflowing, and there were several empty liquor bottles all over the floor. Aunt Kathy did her best to clear a path as she moved through the wreck of a room when something on the floor caught her attention. She bent over and picked up a large envelope that had David's name on it. However, she didn't realize the floor was wet and slipped, falling onto her backside. Relieved she wasn't hurt and a little embarrassed, she quickly stood. As she tried to get up she looked at her palms and noticed they were red. It was then that she realized it was blood. The floor was covered in blood, and she screamed from horror. Her heart began beating rapidly.

"Oh my God," she screamed. "No, what is this? What is going on?" She stood still holding the contents of the envelope in her hand.

Within seconds she heard footsteps coming down the stairs.

"Is everything alright?" Mrs. Kelly asked.

Aunt Kathy didn't respond. Instead she took a seat on the bed.

"Ms. Benton?" she said, moving toward Aunt Kathy.

Aunt Kathy looked up at the ceiling and tears rolled down her face. She had a bad feeling about this. It started with the shooting, the death of Lauren's boyfriend, and now this. Aunt Kathy had a notion that all of these things were somehow related. She said a silent prayer and then tore the unsealed envelope open. She hoped that whatever was inside would explain whatever was going on. She hoped the answers to all of the madness going on around her were inside.

Aunt Kathy pulled a few pictures out and a note fell to the floor. Mrs. Kelly bent down before her to pick it up and handed it to back to her. Aunt Kathy mouthed a silent thank you and began reading the note. Unfortunately, the note left her even more clueless, so she took a look at the pictures. At first, she couldn't identify the people in the picture, but she could see they were photos of two corpses. Aunt Kathy was left even more confused because she didn't understand why someone would send photographs of dead people to her nephew. She examined the pictures closer for further inspection and as reality of what she was seeing hit her, the pictures fell from her hand one by one. The prints landed face up, and she knew without a doubt that the eyes of the woman in the picture were those of her sister.

41

Jerry

I don't know how long I was unconscious, but it felt like an eternity. When I came to, I didn't even know where the hell I was. I did know, however, that if I ever got loose, a lot of people were going to die. Every time I tried to move, the pain became unbearable. They had me tied to a chair in the middle of a dark room. The only time I caught a glimpse of something was when they came into the room with a lamp to fuck me up. But at that point, I could care less. Once I saw my mother and brother in those pictures, I was completely drained of emotions. Everything I ever did in my life was for my family. Realizing now that they were all gone left me numb inside. I didn't care if I lived or died. I couldn't even cry, and maybe if I did, I could find a way to cope with my situation. All I knew was that if I didn't die soon, I would go crazy.

Chico's goons tried to keep me alive and barely fed me, but I was fueled with adrenaline and anger, which enabled me to hang on. All I needed was the perfect chance to break loose. So many questions were racing through my mind. The one that stuck out most was where my baby sister Loria was. She wasn't in any of the horrible pictures they showed me.

The door opened, and I heard footsteps come toward me. I braced myself for another beating, when suddenly, they stopped. A light came on and I squinted to adjust my eyes. I tried to catch a glimpse of the shadow that was now heading my way.

"Jerry?" a low voice whispered.

I didn't reply.

The person came into the light, and when I saw who it was, my insides boiled with fury. This cock-sucking snitch had the nerve to call my name. A flood of memories came rushing through my head when I realized that it was none other than Fifi.

"I'm sorry for what happened, Jerry," Fifi, said, and I noticed she was carrying a bundle in her arms.

I couldn't even reply. She would surely die if I ever got loose. I never liked this bitch from day one. Now I'd make sure she paid with her life.

"Look, I have a lot more to tell you, but I don't have the time. Chico will be back shortly, and I wanted to show you something before I leave," she said, moving toward me.

I just stared at her with fury in my eyes, not caring to see whatever it was she wanted to show me. I noticed she had gained some weight since the last time I saw her. Suddenly, I caught a glimpse of something that made me look down.

"I know this may sound crazy, but this is yours," she said, removing the blanket from a baby's face.

I focused, still trying to adjust to the inadequate lighting and could barely make out the baby's face. I did notice the family resemblance in her nose and eyes. I didn't know what to feel or think because I was emotionally drained. Suddenly, the baby began to cry.

"Her name is Barbara, and I named her after your mother," she said. Before I could gather my thoughts she abruptly left the room with the child. They went upstairs, and I heard the door shut. All I kept thinking about was the name, Barbara.

42

David

Miami is a crazy place. Britney is a straight freak, and I really didn't know why I brought her with me. My boys told me not to bring sand to the beach. At first, I didn't want to come down to Miami alone, but I soon learned, Miami chicks were down for anything. I had to leave Britney's ass at the hotel a couple of times. She even bitched because I wouldn't take her along with me for my meetings with my connect. Of course, I had to put up with her arguing with me for leaving her alone. She thinks she's my girl—nah, bump that, she thinks she's wifey.

In the beginning we had a nice understanding. I told her that I wasn't looking for a relationship, and it would be best if we kept it at being friends, only with some benefits. She said she was good with that, but that shit went in one ear and out the other. She started getting possessive, wanting to know my every move.

I knew she was catching feelings when she showed up at my school one day wanting to fight with Mrs. Kelly. She had followed my car one day and thought she saw me kissing Mrs. Kelly. Truth be told, Jerry and I had switched cars a couple of times, and she ended up following him instead of me. She's a rider though. I guess that's why she's still around.

A while back, I bumped into the dude I had a fight with at Club Mystique on Jamaica Avenue. At the time, Britney was in Jimmy Jazz buying a pair of sneakers while I waited outside. Anyway, the dude recognized me and started going ballistic, talking about how he was going to kill me and shit. I was so caught up with that fool I didn't even notice Britney come out of the store. She wound up punching this fool in the face and was swinging wildly. This dude then pulled out a knife and tried to stab her. Long story short, we both ended up beating the shit out of him. I went to the hospital because I needed three stitches for a small cut on my lower jaw. I knew after that little episode that Britney was definitely down with me all the way. Still, I needed breathing room.

I snuck out while she was sleeping so I could have some alone time. I didn't know, what was going on with me, but I had been experiencing these mood swings, and it felt odd. The feelings surfaced every time something went wrong. I pulled out my cell phone and dialed Jerry's number, but it went straight into his voice mail, so I tried dialing the house phone.

"Hello," a woman answered.

I looked at the phone to make sure I had the right number and saw that it was correct.

"Who is this?" I asked, not recognizing the voice on the other end.

"Jerry?" the lady asked, becoming excited.

"No, this is David. Who is this?" I asked, losing my patience.

"This is Mrs. Kelly, David. Something happened here, and we can't get in contact with Jerry," she said, sounding distressed.

"What do you mean, something happened? Where is my aunt—I mean my mother?" I asked, now becoming worried.

"She's right here. Hold on."

A few seconds went by, then my aunt got on the phone.

"Aunt Kathy, what's going on?" I asked.

"Everything is wrong. I think something happened to your brother," she said, crying. She explained what she had found and what had happened in Haiti. "I'm so, so sorry," she said, crying uncontrollably.

Everything began moving in slow motion. I started thinking about the past—and all the good and bad times my family and I had together, and how I never got a chance to show them all the good life outside of Haiti. We were going to wait until things cooled down before sending for them. I started to cry my heart out. I couldn't understand who would do that to them. Then it suddenly it hit me like a ton of bricks. I hadn't thought that there might be repercussions, after robbing that piece of shit. All I could see was the money and the chance to come to the States. My past was now back to haunt me, and it felt as though my life was crumbling before my eyes. If it was the last thing I did, I was going to kill Chico for what he did to my family.

"What did the note say?" I finally asked after calming down a little. "It said something about the Grim Reaper, and it was signed, your buddy, Mario."

"Mario?" I repeated.

The only Mario I knew was dead.

"Shit!" I said, thinking out loud.

How the hell did Chico find us?

"Did you call the police?" I asked.

"No. I was waiting to speak with you first," Aunt Kathy said.

"Okay, good. I will get to the bottom of what is going on before we contact the police," I said.

"Listen, David, I don't know what you and your brother are mixed up in, but you two need to stop! You didn't come to America to cause trouble or get killed. I already lost a nephew, niece, and a sister, and I don't want to lose any more of my family. Things are different here. This is not Haiti. The police will not hesitate to kill you or lock you up. Don't think for a second, just because you are light skinned and have gray eyes that they will show you favors. You'll never be able to fit in— history will prove that to you. They are waiting for young black men just like you to mess up. That's what they expect. I don't know where your brother is, and I pray to God that he's okay," she said, sounding very emotional.

"Okay, Aunt Kathy. Please put Mrs. Kelly back on the phone. I love you," I said before she handed over the phone.

"I love you too, baby," she said, sniffling.

Mrs. Kelly came back on the line.

"Listen, make sure my mother is doing alright. If anyone asks you, you don't know where I am. Don't talk to anyone about this. Stay in touch with any news. Be available at all costs," I said.

"Okay. Please let me know if you need anything."

"Alright. Talk to you later," I said and hung up the phone.

I needed to assemble the crew. We needed a strategy to tackle this new situation.

After pulling myself together, I decided to make a call.

"Hello."

"Yo, this is Major," I said, pacing back and forth.

"Yo, they got Block and Ricky. They just called me from central booking and told me they're getting locked up for murder!" Gully said in Creole.

"Shit!" I said. This situation was getting worse by the minute. First Jerry, now this. Our plans were beginning to unravel.

"They said they were followed that night."

"Listen, I need you to get the fuck out of your crib. We can't even be on the phones, so I'll be sending you something to your wife's house. Be on point, son. Things are about to get thick, alright," I warned, speaking in Creole.

"Haitians4Life."

"Haitians4Life."

43

Ricky

Rikers Island

Block and Ricky were at Riker's Island after being held at the precinct for almost eighteen hours. They were separated and housed in different facilities. Block was in George Motchan Detention Center, and Ricky was placed in Adolescent Retention and Detention Center. Ricky was in his cell trying to get some sleep.

All night long, these motherfuckers have been arguing. I can't even take a nap. My borough this, my borough that. One asshole even had the audacity to brag that he was from Queens and was getting money from Major and King. Dude wasn't even Haitian, Ricky thought, laughing to himself.

Ricky knew everyone who was getting money from the Body Snatchers. They had over twenty dudes rolling with them. Even though King and Major stopped dealing drugs, they had others handling that business for them.

With nothing else to do but wait, Ricky's thoughts started to drift. He began thinking about his present predicament and his mother. A few months ago, his mother went to Haiti to visit a sick family member. Everyone was happy to see her because his mother was loved by the community. It wasn't long before word spread that she was back in town. During her previous visit to Haiti she had some financial issues and borrowed money from someone. She returned to the States shortly thereafter without paying off her debt. When the loan shark heard she returned he sent for her and she was never seen or heard from again.

He overheard his father and uncle talking one evening and learned the person responsible for his mother's death was a devious man named Chico.

Ricky loved his mother, and her death made him despondent, and he was filled with raw hatred. His mother was the one person who kept their family together, and since her death their family was on the verge of falling apart. Now all Ricky could think about was revenge.

Ricky was staring at the ceiling when the cell door opened. He hopped out of the bed quickly, expecting the worse. The C.O.'s were down with half the crooked activity that went on in the prison.

"Baptiste, legal visit!" the C.O. yelled

"Yeah, alright," he replied.

Gully must have sent the word out to everyone and got me a lawyer, he thought.

"I'm ready," Ricky said, following the C.O.

"Come get your pass," the C.O. demanded.

"Alright."

Ricky was wearing a gray prison jumpsuit. Normally, prisoners were allowed to wear regular clothes, but it was mandatory to wear the jumpsuits during visits. This was a necessary precaution to help the C.O.'s differentiate the prisoners from visitors.

The door opened, and a woman walked in wearing shades and a wide-brimmed hat. She closed the door and stood before Ricky, then she removed the hat and glasses.

"Oh shit!" Ricky said, surprised to see Mrs. Kelly.

"Hey, Ricky," she said smiling before taking a seat.

Mrs. Kelly donned a navy blue pinstriped suit and was wearing a red camisole beneath it, showing off her ample cleavage. Her hair looked as if she just strolled out of a beauty salon. She wore a pair of pearl earrings along with a matching necklace that rested on top of her full breasts. Ricky began daydreaming about all the things he could do to Mrs. Kelly sexually. Then her voice jarred him back to reality.

"How are you doing, Mr. Baptiste?" she asked, winking at Ricky.

"You a lawyer now, huh?" Ricky asked, smiling.

"It is my part-time hustle, if you know what I mean," she said, winking again. "Everyone sends their love. We have a lot to talk about," she said, her tone turning serious.

"What are you talking about?" Ricky asked, not understanding where this was leading.

"Listen, Major sent me here to talk to you. Something has happened to King," Mrs. Kelly said, sighing.

"What you mean, something happened to King?" he asked, making a face.

"Major didn't go into detail, but it had something to do with their past. He said he needs to know what's going on with you and Block."

Ricky just stared at her for a moment because he wasn't sure what to tell her. He knew she wouldn't have gone through all of this trouble if one of them hadn't sent her.

Sensing his uneasiness, she said, "It's okay. He said that you can trust me."

Ricky hesitated for a moment before deciding to tell the information she needed to take back to Major.

"Apparently during the drop-off, we were followed."

"What drop-off?" she asked.

"Don't worry, he'll get it. Anyway, they locked me and Block up that same night. Block is in C-95. They didn't take us straight to central booking. They separated us and took us to the precinct where we were both interrogated. I don't think they really know shit. That Chink cop, Detective Lang, kept asking about the twins and what part they played in this. He said they had somebody who witnessed us making the drop. I doubt that they have a witness. They probably making that shit up! And if there is such a witness—nah, scratch that, the witness probably is the detective, now that I think about it. That detective knew too many details. As a matter of fact, the way he asked questions and explained the way things went down, that nigga had to have been there. He even asked about the shooting at their house and what I knew about it," Ricky explained.

Mrs. Kelly was overwhelmed with all of the news, but she maintained her composure. She sighed and said, "Major said for you to remain cool. He knows you're official and that you're his body, whatever the hell that means. Also, he's gonna need everyone involved because if King doesn't return soon, summer is gonna be real hot."

Ricky smiled and said, "Cool."

"I won't be back to see you again, but an attorney will be by tomorrow. You should be expecting some clothes, money, and sneakers. You know who to stay in contact with if you need anything. Oh, he also said he'll send you a shorty to keep you company, and she'll be bringing you something," she said, winking.

She picked up her briefcase and stood to leave.

"Can I ask you for a quick favor, Mrs. Kelly?"

"Sure."

"Are you able to be my personal tutor? I need one-on-one personal attention," Ricky said, grinning from ear to ear.

"Boy, you better ask that girl that's coming to see you for help," she said, grabbing the doorknob and smiled.

"Seriously though, tell him I said, Haitians4Life."

"Oh yeah, he told me to tell you Haitians4Life, too," she said as she opened the door and disappeared.

44

Agent Joseph

As long as Agent Joseph could remember he wanted to become a policeman. He used to stay up at night and watch programs like *Cops, NYPD Blue,* and other law enforcement dramas. Although he was born a citizen of the United States, he still considered himself to be Haitian. He had frequented Haiti a lot over the years and was always interested in the history of his culture because he loved it. He would go to war for Haiti if he had to. Haiti suffered from poverty because of the corrupt and greedy government. The politician and government official used the economic funds for their own personal projects, which didn't benefit the economy or its people. The police are corrupt and often would terrorize small businesses and extort them out of their hard-earned money. The people never have a fair chance to prosper, and the government made sure it stayed that way.

Even the people jailed in America have better living conditions than some poor people in Haiti. Prisoners in the U.S. can have a commissary, attend festivals, and are permitted trailer visits, TVs, and a whole bunch of other benefits that were considered luxuries. In Haitian jails, people went weeks without eating. Most people had to rely on their family to provide them with food. Everyone was crowded into cells, and buckets served as toilets. If an individual was killed or died the body wouldn't be removed until a guard felt like doing it or the body began to decompose. Life in Haiti was rough all around.

After Agent Camper fouled up with the ransom, Agent Joseph became lead investigator of the Body Snatchers case. Media was all over this case given the fact that the governor's son had been killed.

Agent Joseph had just given the director and governor a summary of the case and what they were dealing with.

"Jesus Henry Christ!" the director exclaimed in astonishment.

"These other guys have prior state convictions, but Jerry and David Benton are both clean as a whistle. Despite their age, I don't believe we're dealing with your average teenagers here," Agent Joseph explained.

"I don't give a flying shit who you believe these thugs are. What I want are those Haitians' heads delivered to me on a silver fucking platter—and now!" the governor yelled.

The director cringed at his statement.

Agent Joseph looked at the governor with contempt in his eyes, and the director knew how antagonistic Agent Joseph could get about his country.

"Gentleman, I have someone new joining the case. He flew in from Haiti at my request. He's considered a close friend and is to be treated as one," the governor said, turning his back from everyone.

"Listen, the FBI has everything under control. I don't need any additional liability on this investigation," Agent Joseph replied haughtily.

The phone rang, disturbing their heated discussion. The director placed the call on speaker and answered. "Savelli, here."

"Director Savelli, you have a visitor by the name of Mr. Alexis. Shall I send him in?" the assistant asked.

"Yes, send him in."

The governor turned around and said, "Right on time."

Agent Joseph looked at the director. "You knew about this?" he asked angrily.

The director tapped his cigar against the ashtray, removing the excess ash and simply blew smoke from his nostrils and shrugged.

The door opened, and a tall, dark-skinned, heavy-set man walked in.

"Good afternoon, gentlemen," he said, smiling.

"I would like you to meet Mr. Daniel Alexis," the governor introduced.

Mr. Alexis walked over and shook Agent Joseph's hand.

"Agent Joseph," he said. "You look rather familiar, Mr. Alexis."

Still shaking hands, he said, "Enough with the formalities. You can call me Chico."

45

Jerry

Fifi had been sneaking down to see me whenever the coast was clear. She brought food and fed me. On occasion, she would bring my daughter to visit. I'm not gonna lie, I started to form a bond with them. She wasn't that bad, after all. We started to talk about a lot of things. Although it hurt me to listen, she even told me about what happened that night we left Haiti. She said she never told Chico what happened, but he figured it out after watching the videotape.

It was still hard to believe I had a daughter. She is so beautiful. I never really thought about having kids. My mind was always on making money, but now, all I could think about was finding a way to get out of here. I knew my mom would have been so happy just to see her granddaughter. Just thinking about it made me cry when I was alone.

While Fifi was feeding me, she noticed that I wasn't really responsive. She stopped once she saw tears running down my cheeks.

"What's wrong?" she asked sympathetically.

"Nothing," I said abruptly.

She just stared at me.

"What?" I asked.

Her eyes filled with tears.

"Why are you still so hateful toward me?" she asked, wiping her face.

I couldn't respond.

"Talk to me," she pleaded.

"Listen, man, what happened was a mistake, alright? What do you expect, a relationship? Whatever happened to you and David?" I asked.

She started crying, then looked away and said, "I know it was a mistake, but you act like I wanted all of this to happen, and I wasn't the one who was being deceitful. I love David, but now you and I have a baby together, and though we never got along, we have to try. If y'all would have told me from the beginning what y'all were planning, then maybe things would've turned out differently."

"Listen, I still haven't told David what happened between us that night. I know he won't be happy about this, but he'll have to understand you had my daughter, and now she's the only family we have left," I explained to her.

"Everything we were working hard for is now gone." I sighed.

Fifi stopped crying. She looked like she was about to say something. Instead she abruptly walked away.

She must be crazy, I thought. What did she really expect to happen between us? Was she expecting that we'd move in together and live happily ever after? I would never do that. I crossed my brother once, never thinking about the consequences, and violated Fifi. Those two things will never happen again. I'm not so sure I should even trust her. She claimed she didn't tell Chico I was the father, but I still had my doubts about that.

Now my main concern was getting out of my present situation and telling my brother about the baby once the smoke clears. There would be no easy way to break the news to David. On more than one occasion I wanted to tell him I had slept with Fifi, but there never seemed to be a good time.

The door opened and Fifi returned. However, now she had someone else with her.

"Oh my God!" I said, overwhelmed with emotions.

"Loria? But how? I asked, confused. "What is she doing here? I thought she was de—" I got choked up after seeing my little sister.

"The night when Chico went to your house looking for y'all, he found the money under your mother's mattress. While he was questioning your mother, Loria snuck out of the house, and I found her out back. I knew she didn't have any other family, so after everything died down I went back and got her. She's been with me ever since."

46

Jerry

Fifi was filled with mixed emotions. She felt horrible about Jerry and David's family, her cousin Mario getting killed, Loria witnessing the murder of her family, and Jerry being tortured day after day. She knew the twins were involved in killing her cousin, but she didn't want anyone else to die. She held so much resentment toward her uncle, and she was now willing to do just about anything, to get back at him.

Prior to the birth of her daughter, she broke down and told uncle Chico that she was pregnant. He didn't even bother to ask her any questions. He was so consumed with anger and plotting revenge, he merely said, "Just stay out of my way." And when her uncle Chico told her they were leaving for the States, she knew it had something to do with David and Jerry, but she also saw a great opportunity to reunite Loria with her brothers and to inform Jerry he was the father of a beautiful baby girl.

Chico left two weeks before Fifi, which gave her the opportunity to gather papers for Loria and purchase her plane ticket. She wasn't concerned about her uncle finding out about Loria because she was planning to tell him that she was Sophie's sister.

Fifi walked downstairs with Loria and slowly approached Jerry. She watched as Loria ran to embrace Jerry and was relieved she hadn't let anything happen to her.

"Loria?" Jerry asked, shocked.

"Jerry!" Loria screamed, running toward her big brother.

Jerry was still handcuffed to the chair and couldn't hug Loria, but she sat on his lap and wrapped her arms around him. Fifi could hear the sniffling and soft sobs coming from him. Fifi wanted badly to join in, but she knew he needed time alone with his sister. Fifi realized although she loved David, she was also in love with Jerry. She was in denial at first because they had never gotten along. David was smart, calm, and easy to talk to. Jerry, on the other hand, was a live wire, unpredictable, and had this mysteriousness about him that she found irresistible.

"Are you okay?" Jerry softly asked Loria.

"The bad men hurt Mommy and Johnny!" she said, wiping her tears with the back of her hands.

"I know," he said, crying. "I know, but they didn't do anything to hurt you, huh, sweetie?" Jerry asked.

"No, they didn't. Fifi is taking care of me."

Jerry looked at Fifi and said, "You saved her life. Thank you."

Just then, they heard footsteps, and the door swung open. Joey, one of Chico's new recruits, stormed into the room.

"What the hell you doing down here?" he barked, stomping toward Fifi.

"Nothing, I was ju—" Fifi managed to say before he grabbed her by her ponytail. "Get the fuck off me!" Fifi yelled, trying to fight him off. She turned toward him and bit into his arm as hard as she could.

He yelled, throwing Fifi to the ground.

He turned and kicked her in the stomach.

"Fuck you doing?" Jerry shouted, fighting against the restraints.

Joey walked over to him and punched him in the mouth.

"Let me go!" Loria screamed, trying to hold on to Jerry.

"Let her go, you piece of shit! I swear, I'm gonna kill your ass!" Jerry hollered.

Pulling out his gun, Joey ordered Fifi out of the room. She looked at Jerry and saw something in his eyes that scared her even more than the gun in Joey's hand. The darkness and coldness in his eyes told her the man before her was capable of anything.

He gave Fifi a nod and slowly she rose to her feet and grabbed Loria without looking back. It was then that she made a decision to help Jerry escape no matter what the price.

47

David

My world was fucked up! Ricky and Block were in jail. Aunt Kathy's house was hot, and the local police and the feds had my aunt's phones tapped. Worst of all, nobody knows where my brother is. Everyone had their ears to the street, but no one could come up with shit. But if I didn't get some news soon, a lot of those motherfuckers were going to die.

Gully's girl, Meena, had a house in Rosedale, and it was located on the border of Long Island and Queens. Meena was quiet and also a loner, so less than a handful of people knew about her or her whereabouts. I didn't have to worry about anyone finding us there. I decided to stay there, ever since my return from Miami. I hadn't seen or spoken to Britney since, and she was blowing up my phone day and night. I didn't have time for her right now. I couldn't risk taking any more chances because too many people had seen her with me. The FBI was all over the place, knocking on too many doors and asking questions about Jerry and me. I had no doubt that by now they had gotten to her and were watching her every step, and that told me two things. One, I had to cut off all ties until things died down, and two, they didn't have a clue as to where Jerry was, so they probably assumed we were together.

I sparked a blunt I had in the ashtray and watched Gully pace. He'd been doing that for the past hour. Everyone's nerves were on edge, and we barely slept. The clock was still ticking, yet so much still had to be done. I leaned back in my chair, tilted my head back, and stared at the ceiling. I recently learned that the feds had picked up Block and Ricky's case and were transferring them to a federal penitentiary. I took a long drag from my blunt and inhaled the smoke as though it would be my last one.

"What we gonna do?" Gully asked.

Silence filled the air.

A wave of emotions ran through me—rage, sorrow, regret, and anxiety. I felt sorrow because I saw what would happen in my future and that there was the possibility that it may even lead to my death. I also felt regret for all the things I never got to do or say to my family. I felt rage because people who were close to me were now either in danger or dead. A lone tear ran down my cheek.

"Yo, Gully!" I said, surprised to hear my own voice.

"Yeah?" he responded.

I could sense he was watching me. Still staring at the ceiling, I answered, "Get everyone together. We're gonna make our move."

48

Ricky

Ricky sent word to Major that he and Block would be picked up by the feds in about two weeks, but they never responded. The last that Ricky heard from anyone was when he saw Mrs. Kelly, and from what he'd been told, Block hadn't heard anything either. However, they did send him a PYT—the pretty young thing he was promised.

Geneva's eyes were like black pearls that could mesmerize any man. Her almond-shaped eyes were flanked with long, lustrous lashes. Her skin was the color of a copper penny with a metallic rose colored tint to her cheeks. Her shoulder-length hair fell loosely over her shoulders into spiral curls. Geneva's innocent face emulated a quiet, honest demeanor, yet her body was lethal and could cause a multiple car pileup. Ricky loved everything about her, but mostly the fact that Geneva proved to be a ryder.

Geneva and Ricky attended school together, and their paths crossed several times, but nothing serious ever happened. Geneva claimed she always had a thing for Ricky, and when she heard he was incarcerated, she got in contact with his boys to get his info. She was the only one who visited Ricky, ever since Mrs. Kelly. She sent letters, gave him money, accepted his collect calls, and proved to be loyal. Ricky decided that when or if, he ever got out, he was definitely going to make her his woman.

Block and Ricky were being transferred to a federal penitentiary in Virginia. They were transported in separate cars, including three agents serving as escorts. Seated in the third car were Detective Lang and his partner. Ricky took in the sights of the streets as they drove past the criminal courthouse on Queens Boulevard. The way things were going, he didn't know if he'd ever see or enjoy the outside world again. He hadn't heard from King or Major since he got knocked, and the only thing keeping him sane at this point was Geneva. As usual, traffic was moving at a steady pace. As the car that Ricky occupied paused for a red light, an advertisement on the side of a bus caught his attention. A second later a garbage truck pulled up alongside them, blocking Ricky's view altogether.

"You guys seemed to cause quite a ruckus," the fat white agent said from the passenger seat, gaining Ricky's attention.

"Is that so?" Ricky replied sarcastically.

"Joseph, what did they call themselves again?" he asked the agent who was driving.

"Body Snatchers," Agent Joseph said.

"Should have called them Booty Scratchers!" the fat white agent bellowed.

"That's enough," Agent Joseph said.

The light turned green, and the car began moving again. When they passed the garbage truck, Ricky glanced at the driver and was startled. Then he inadvertently looked at the agent with a dumbstruck look.

"Fuck wrong with you?" the agent riding next to Ricky asked, making a face.

"Ain't shit wrong with me," Ricky answered with an attitude regaining his compsure.

Turning the corner, the car switched lanes in order to get onto the highway. The car picked up speed as it approached the on ramp. Once again, Ricky noticed the garbage truck trying to catch up to the car. As the truck passed the car, Ricky zoomed in on the driver.

"Oh, shit! Bones. I'm not going crazy," Ricky mumbled to himself.

"What did you say?" the agent asked.

"Damn, you lonely or something? I wasn't talking to you," Ricky said, getting annoyed.

"Well, shut the fuck up then," the agent countered.

"Yeah, alright."

"We'll see how tough you are once we drop you off," he said, chuckling.

Ignoring him, Ricky returned his attention to the garbage truck that had now switched lanes and was in front of them. He noticed something else, too. The agent driving the car tried to get from behind the truck, but a school bus was blocking their passage. Suddenly they were surrounded by a swarm of roaring engines.

"Will you look at this shit here," the fat agent said, staring out his window.

Ricky turned to look at what caught the agent's attention.

A row of red and blue motorcycles trailed one another in biker fashion. There were seven of them in total. Four of them had passengers. All of them wore motorcycle jackets that matched their bikes, all designed to look like the Haitian flag.

"What is this asshole doing?" Agent Joseph asked, banging on the car horn in frustration.

The garbage truck slowed down, causing all the other cars to follow suit. The school bus and motorcycles made it impossible to switch lanes.

Suddenly someone jumped out of the rear of the garbage truck, causing trash bags to litter the roadway. The masked man aimed a shotgun in their direction, blasting a shot through the car's front window. The bullet hit the fat agent like a bull's-eye in the forehead.

"Oh shit!" Ricky screamed, ducking down in his seat.

Blood and brain matter splattered throughout the car and landed on Ricky. Agent Joseph slammed on the brakes. Gunshots were being fired from all directions. Another car rear ended them, causing Ricky to lurch forward and bump his head into the headrest of the passenger seat. Ricky quickly sat up and saw a biker pull up and fire a hail of bullets into the second agent's body, making his body dance and fall on top of Ricky's lap. Using the advantage of being handcuffed from the front, he pushed the agent off him and searched his pockets for the keys. Ricky jumped when he heard a moan.

"You alright back there?" Agent Joseph asked in Creole.

Ricky was taken aback by the fact that Agent Joseph spoke in Creole.

"You alright?" he asked again, this time turning around.

"Yeah," Ricky replied.

Ricky was so busy trying to locate the handcuff keys he didn't notice the sledgehammer slamming into his window, shattering the glass like crushed ice. The door opened and Major smiled down at Ricky.

"You didn't think I'd leave you?" Major asked.

"Nah," Ricky said, smiling.

"Come on. We gotta go," Major said, helping Ricky out of the car.

"Where's Block?" Ricky asked, looking around for him.

His smile faded, and he shook his head. Block was now a casualty of war.

"Don't move!" Agent Joseph yelled in Creole, pointing his gun at Ricky and Major.

He opened the driver's side door and got out, still aiming his gun at them.

However, he was outnumbered as Jinx came around to the side of the car, aiming his shotgun directly at Agent Joseph's head.

"Put your fucking gun down now before I give you a face-lift, nigga!" Jinx demanded.

Agent Joseph slowly dropped his gun on the ground and raised both his hands in the air.

"What you want me to do?" Jinx asked.

Major stared at the agent, sizing him up before giving his order. "Leave him."

"You sure?"

"Yeah. Come on. Let's go!"

A black Suburban screeched to a stop next to the guys and the back door opened. They ran to the car and hopped in. The motorcycles roared passed them, and a couple of them were popping wheelies. The car sped off, following the motorcycles.

Ricky turned around to take a look at the crime scene and saw Block's head leaning out of the car window.

"Haitians4Life, my nigga," Ricky whispered. "Haitians4Life."

49

Agent Joseph

gent Joseph walked away with minor injuries. He sustained a minor concussion, neck sprain, and scratches to his face. He was given extra-strength Tylenol for his migraine and ordered to go home and rest, but Agent Joseph had no intention of resting.

The prisoners' escape made international headlines. Jamaica Hospital was surrounded with reporters. The FBI had to shut down the hospital emergency door alarms in order for Agent Joseph to leave the the premises undetected.

Agent Joseph knew he was lucky to be alive. The ambush happened so quickly, he had no time to react. However, prior to the incident he felt extremely tense, and when he saw the bikers, his antennas went up. The Haitian flag jacket and the flag hanging from the back pocket of a female passenger caught his attention immediately. Before he could act on his suspicions, the fatal shot was fired. Agent Joseph stepped on the brakes, and everything after that was pure mayhem. He'd been involved in gun battles before, but nothing like what occurred yesterday on the Van Wyck Expressway. His heart never raced that fast as he saw his life flash before him. Still, he'd never know why his life was spared.

Stepping into the director's office, Agent Joseph braced himself for the inevitable.

"Holy Mackerel! Mother of Red Lobsters!" he yelled, raising his hands up to the ceiling.

Chico stood near the window as the director went off on a tirade.

Agent Joseph merely grabbed a seat and listened.

"A simple task of transporting, and you guys managed to make the papers! Can you explain to me how transferring two friggin' prisoners led to a damn highway massacre? Please explain, because I just don't get it! Go ahead because I can't wait to hear your explanation!" the director shouted, waving his hands frantically.

Agent Joseph gave his account of what happened, but intentionally omitted the part about the bikers allowing him to walk free.

"These assholes are really starting to embarrass us," the director said, drumming his fingers on the desk.

The director had a habit of switching back and forth between English and Italian, especially when he was angry.

Agent Joseph peered over at Chico who wore this nonchalant expression.

Agent Joseph was curious to learn exactly what was going on with this guy and still couldn't understand why he was even there. As it stood, Chico hadn't said or brought anything useful to the table yet.

"The two people worth investigating at this point are David and Jerry, the twins," he said.

"Why?" Agent Joseph asked, frowning.

"I'm getting to that. Legally, there is no data verifying their entry into the United States. The information retrieved from their school records show no educational background prior to them enrolling into this Satellite Learning Center. They just appeared out of nowhere and started attending school in January 2000. I don't believe any of the incidents are coincidental, but all somehow related. There was an incident in Florida earlier this year. My resources tell me a boat had been stopped while illegally docking in Oyster Cove, and it was filled with Haitians. In the midst of this, Haitians began jumping overboard and the coast guards opened fire. Eight Haitians were killed along with two coast guards. In one of the reports I read where a guard spotted two men who managed to escape. What stood out was that he listed the men were identical in appearance," Chico said matter-of-factly, picking the dirt out from under his nails.

"If you don't mind me asking, what is it that you do over in Haiti?" Agent Joseph asked.

"No, I don't mind. I'm what you would call a political consultant," Chico said, turning to face Agent Joseph.

Political consultant, huh? What the hell does that entail? Agent Joseph thought.

Chico's cell phone rang, and he looked down at the screen and took the call. "Excuse me, gentlemen, but I have to take this," he said, stepping out of the office.

"I don't trust him," Agent Joseph said to the director.

The director nodded and said, "He is kind of strange, but the governor brought him on for a reason."

"So what's next?" Agent Joseph asked.

"The police commissioner and the governor will go before the press. As for us, there's a microscope so far up our asses, they can see what we ate for breakfast. As for that guy, I don't know. He's the governor's problem, not mine. I just need you to make sure he doesn't compromise this investigation."

Agent Joseph nodded.

"You're walking on thin ice right now, so you need to be very careful. I'm getting a lot of shit from the guys upstairs, and right now I need to assure them we have everything under control. I need you to come up with a plan, pronto! Capeesh?"

The door opened, and Chico reentered the room.

"I'm sorry, but something just came up that requires my immediate attention. I'll keep you informed on my progress. I'll be in touch," he said, leaving with a sense of urgency.

Agent Joseph looked at the director as he leaned back in his chair and matched the expression on Agent Joseph's face.

Agent Joseph got up to follow suit and leave as he figured his business was done there.

"Joseph," the director called out.

"Yeah."

"Thin ice."

Agent Joseph nodded and left.

50

David

We got Ricky back, but lost Block in the process. The car he was riding in flipped over several times and was crushed by a truck. We saw the car crushed on its side off the highway. I knew there was always a possibility that something like this could happen, but this changed a lot of things. The bar had been raised now, and there was no going back. From now on, everything would have to be done to our best and to the extreme.

I sent the money Block had saved to his family. Hopefully, they accept it. I picked up a prepaid cell phone and began to dial.

"St. Mary Immaculate Hospital," a woman answered.

"Yes, this is Mr. Jack Krosby of the Department of the Haitian Embassy. Is Ms. Benton available?" I asked.

"Hold on, please."

I wondered what kind of look she would have on her face, once they told her it was the Haitian Embassy trying to reach her.

"Hello?" a skeptical voice answered.

"Ms. Benton?"

"Yes."

"Hey, Aunt Kathy."

There was silence.

"Do you know how much trouble you're in?" she asked, worry coating her voice.

"Yes, I do."

"The police are all over my house. Every time I look out the window, I see people watching. Lauren and I are worried sick about the both of you."

"I know, and that's why I decided to call and let you know that I'm fine."

"Did you find your brother?"

"No. You didn't tell anybody about what happened, did you?"

"No, but a girl called and left me a message. She said that Mario's father has Jerry, and that Loria is still alive."

"What?" I yelled, sitting down now.

"She also said that he's working as an investigator and he's searching for you. David, I don't have a good feeling about all of this. Why don't you just turn yourself in, before someone else gets hurt?" Aunt Kathy lamented.

I ignored her comment. "Is that everything?"

Aunt Kathy let out an exasperated sigh before replying, "Yes."

"Did this girl leave a name?"

"Yes, she did."

"What is it?"

"Fifi."

51

A letter was left at Director Savelli's office, and it was from the Body Snatchers, but this letter had Director Savelli a little confused and even frightened. The director had a hard time deciphering what was in the letter because it was written in either French or Creole. He had to ask Agent Joseph to translate the letter, which made Director Savelli even more confused. He looked down to read the translated report once again:

YOU HAVE SOMETHING WE WANT. YOU WILL RECEIVE A CALL ON THE TENTH, AT 4:00 P.M. THERE WILL BE NO FURTHER NEGOTIATIONS. IF OUR DEMANDS ARE NOT MET, YOU WILL HAVE TO DEAL WITH THE REPERCUSSIONS.
—THE BODY SNATCHERS

"Jabones Pazzo, crazy assholes," Director Savelli mumbled. "I'm getting too old for this shit. What the hell are they asking for? These guys are psycho terrorists."

The phone rang, pulling him from his reverie.

"Savelli!" the director barked into the phone.

"Agent Camper is here and requests to speak to you, sir."

"What does this guy want?" Director Savelli mumbled under his breath, getting even more frustrated.

"What was that, sir?"

"Send him in," Director Savelli replied just as abruptly as he hung up.

Director Savelli started placing all the reports into a folder and filed them in his desk drawer. He leaned back in his chair and watched Agent Camper walk in. He hadn't seen Agent Camper since he fucked up and caused the death of the governor's son. The agency suspended Agent Camper indefinitely until they determined if he should return at all. Director Savelli folded his hands over his stomach and nodded for him to have a seat.

"How's life been treating you?" Director Savelli asked, eyeing Agent Camper sharply.

Agent Camper disliked small talk. He was a straight shooter. This was a quality that Director Savelli admired about him. But occasionally, Agent Camper was a know-it-all and a bit too cocky for his own good, which was exactly what caused Agent Camper to get thrown off the current case.

Agent Camper sat down and got straight down to business, informing Director Savelli what he'd been up to since his suspension.

"I've been doing a little snooping around and stumbled upon some powerful information that could be helpful in the Body Snatchers case," Agent Camper said, leaning forward in his seat.

"Have you been watching the news lately?" Director Savelli asked.

"Yes, sir," Agent Camper said, frowning.

Director Savelli reached for the gold case on top of his desk and took out a cigar.

"You realize that this isn't one of those cases where you can pull your James Bond stunts," the director warned, toying with the cigar between his fingers.

"Yes, sir," Agent Camper replied.

"Last I checked, you've been on a pretty long vacation," Director Savelli said, pointing his cigar at Agent Camper who did not respond to the comment. Instead he continued to speak.

"Last week, I decided to check up on a couple of leads I thought were imperative to the case. I spoke to Detective Lang, the officer who arrested the two guys who were accused of dropping the governor's son into the garbage bin. He suggested that I look into investigating Jerry and David Benton, a set of twins. They have no priors, but he feels strongly that they are somehow connected to the Body Snatchers, or at least knew something about it."

The director nodded and motioned for Agent Camper to continue.

"I followed the twin's mother around and noticed that she was always meeting with another woman. I decided to follow the other woman and also asked a couple of questions about her around the neighborhood. I found out this woman is a teacher, and her name is Sharon Kelly. And get this: she's a teacher at the school the twins attend. I thought it was rather unusual that a teacher would be so friendly with her students' parents. I did a little bit more digging and heard a few rumors, that she allegedly had been sleeping with one of the twins. Mrs. Kelly and I had a talk. I questioned her about the rumors and asked about her relationship with the Benton family."

"Let me understand you correctly: You cornered a civilian and questioned her on accusations that you had no proof of, and you didn't even show a badge?" the director asked, staring him directly in the eyes.

Agent Camper shifted nervously in his seat.

"And all you did was question her, right?" Director Savelli asked again, feeling a little skeptical.

"Yes, sir."

The director knew he was lying. He had heard Agent Camper's interrogations before, and he knew if you were under this line of questioning without an attorney present, it was lights out first and then he'd give you your rights.

"Go ahead," Director Savelli said.

"She wasn't cooperative at first. She claimed she was a friend of the family, and that was all. Then I told her I had pictures of her and one of the twins in a compromising situation and that I would send it to the local news and inform them about her student-teacher affair. She was a little more responsive after I told her that, and although she didn't openly admit to the affair, she did tell me something interesting. She stated that Jerry had been kidnapped by some guy who came to the States and had a vendetta against the twins, but they didn't have any idea where he was located."

"Did she tell you who this guy was?" the director asked, taking it all in. He glanced around the room as he started to pull some possible ideas together.

"Yeah."

"Well?" Director Savelli said anxiously.

"Apparently, she doesn't know the guy's real name, but she overheard the mother speaking to the daughter about a man named Chico, or something along those lines."

Director Savelli now sat up in his seat. Agent Camper had his full attention because he couldn't believe his ears.

"Say that again?" Director Savelli asked making sure he wasn't hearing things.

"She said she thinks his name is Chico. I did some additional digging on Chico and found out he's some big drug lord in Haiti and has a lot of connections. The Haitian authorities have been trying to bring him down for a long time now, but they could never seem connect him to anything illegal," Agent Camper said.

Director Savelli grabbed the phone and dialed the receptionist's desk.

"Yes, Director Savelli," the voice answered.

"Get Agent Joseph on the line, and tell him to haul his ass down here, pronto." *Now I kind of understand what the letter is about. Somehow they must've figured out that Chico is working on the case. We're about to take these wannabe bad boys down.* He thought.

52

Agent Joseph

They hadn't made much progress on the case thus far, and Agent Joseph searched for clues day and night. The case had him drained, and he hadn't had a good night's rest since. The sun was just beginning to rise, and he found himself already reporting to duty.

He entered the director's office and wasn't surprised at seeing Agent Camper there.

"Morning, gentlemen," he said, grabbing a seat next to Agent Camper.

They greeted each other.

"Have a seat," the director said. "Camper decided to open his own investigation on the Body Snatchers, even though his ass is suspended," the director said, looking intently at Agent Camper.

"He got some groundbreaking information that could possibly crack this case wide open. He received a tip to follow Jerry and David Benton, the twins who are believed to be part of the Body Snatchers. In doing so, Agent Camper learned that one of the twins, Jerry Benton, was kidnapped. After further investigation of Mrs. Sharon Kelly, a teacher at the Satellite Learning Center, Agent Camper learned Jerry Benton has been kidnapped by a guy who goes by the name of Chico. I'm almost positive this is the same Chico who arrived from Haiti to assist the governor with his son's kidnapping case," the director stated, leaning back in his chair.

"Political consultant," Agent Joseph said, chuckling.

"I knew it. There was something about him that just didn't sit right with me. After our conversation the other day, I made some inquiries of my own. I called a friend in Haiti who is on the police force about Chico. He said he knew of a Chico and that he was crooked as a crowbar. He said Chico is a leader in an organized crime family, but his political ties have kept him protected. The Haitian government has been trying to connect him to several incidents for a while, but hadn't any luck."

"So, what are we going do now?" Agent Camper asked.

"We're going to kill two birds with one stone. We'll catch the Body Snatchers and bring Chico in for kidnapping, and whatever else we can find on him." Director Savelli continued, "We will send an anonymous tip to David telling him we know where Chico is hiding his brother, then watch the chips fall into place."

"You're serious?" Agent Camper asked, shaking his head. "This may cause us even more problems."

"I don't think that's a good idea," Agent Joseph said, agreeing with Agent Camper.

"Yes, it is. I'm tired of having these assholes terrorizing the community. We had two of those guys in custody, and we lost them. I lost five agents to their one. My instincts tell me they're a little pissed off right now. This is the first solid lead we've had. I want these clowns off the streets. Better them than us," the director said, looking tired.

"Next steps?" Agent Joseph asked.

"Get these bastards and hang them all by the nuts!" the director instructed and sent them on their way.

53

David

While sitting in Gully's girlfriend Meena's living room, I couldn't help but think about the highway bust. That shit was crazy, and it was like being in an action movie. Bullets flew everywhere, and cars flew in the air and twirled like toys and hit the ground with such force they blew up. When the agent crawled out of his car and told us to freeze, I thought for sure that it was over. Just then Gully showed up with his Tek and he was about to blow the agent's head off, but I stopped him. At the time, I wasn't sure exactly why, but there was something familiar about him, especially when I looked into his eyes. It was as though I was looking into the eyes of someone I knew from my past. I needed to find out who this agent was. My thoughts were distracted once Gully walked into the house.

"Yo, Major. What's up?" Gully said, giving me dap.

"Nothing much, man. I was just thinking about all this shit that's going down around us. Was that letter delivered to the director of the FBI?" I asked.

"Yeah, man, just as we planned," Gully responded.

"A'ight, bet."

I got up and walked down to the basement to get a box of newspaper clippings and information on the Body Snatchers case. I looked for the number to call if you had any tips on the case, and I took out my prepaid phone and dialed.

"Hello, tip hotline. How may I help you?" a woman asked.

"Hello. I have a tip about the Body Snatcher case and would like to speak to someone in charge," I said.

"Okay, sir, I'll connect you to the department that is handling this case. Please hold."

"Okay, but before you transfer me, can you tell me if this is the office located in Quantico?"

"Yes it is, sir. Will that be all?" the operator asked.

"Yes, thank you," I said

The operator then connected me to Quantico, where I was transferred to Agent Joseph's office.

"Agent Joseph," he said, answering his phone.

I decided to test him and have the conversation with him in Creole to get a feel of where his head was, and to see if he still had his Haitian pride.

"Bonjour, Agent Joseph," I said, pausing. "I have important information on one of the members of the Body Snatchers. I would like to meet with you at an undisclosed location to discuss this further. I'll need your cell number to call so I can give you the address once the arrangements have been made. Also, if you want to know why you didn't die that day on the highway, I suggest you come alone."

"Who is this?" Agent Joseph demanded, responding in Creole.

"Do you want the information or not?" I asked.

Agent Joseph hesitated for what felt like five minutes, but was probably only ten seconds. I was beginning to lose my patience.

"Do you want this information or not?" I repeated.

"Okay. My cell number is 646-555-1253," he responded.

"Expect a call from me soon," I replied before hanging up the phone.

Okay, maybe now we stood a chance. I thought he wasn't going to respond in Creole, but he did, which showed that he'd be somewhat compliant. Now all I had to do was find a secluded place to meet him, but I would leave that up to Gully. That was his area of expertise.

When I walked into the kitchen, I saw Ricky, Jinx, and Gully talking with their heads together. It looked like they were plotting or setting up a scheme.

"What y'all niggas up to in here?" I questioned.

"Yo, son, we're starving, and there's nothing to eat but junk food in here," Jinx responded.

"We're trying to get this Hamburger Helper popping," Gully said, looking at the back of the box to see how to cook macaroni.

"Did any one of you geniuses figure it out yet?" I asked, laughing.

"Yo, fuck you, son. It was either this or corned beef. We all decided on Hamburger Helper," Jinx responded.

"I suggested we order Chinese food, but Gully said he was tired of eating ching-chong food and wanted to be Chef-Boy-R-homeboy here," Jinx said, laughing hysterically.

Everyone in the room burst out laughing because they all knew how much Gully loved to eat and that he would try cooking just about anything.

"Let me know when y'all niggas figure out how to open the box." I chuckled. "Yo, Gully, I need a spot. I'm going to meet up with Agent Joseph," I said.

"Is that the same agent who was at the highway shootout you allowed to live?" Gully asked, looking up from reading the instructions on the box.

"Yo, that nigga is Haitian. He spoke to me in Creole when we were in the car," Ricky said, opening a bag of chips.

"You think he could help us find Jerry since we know Chico is disguised as a cop," Jinx said, rubbing his beard.

"Yeah, that and something else," I replied, walking to the refrigerator.

"He may be the missing link that we're looking for. Gully, do your thing and find us a location for us to link up," I said, taking a sip of soda.

"A'ight. Consider it done. I have the perfect spot for you up in Westchester," Gully said, rubbing his palms together.

"Cool. I'm going to set up the meeting right now," I said and walked into the living room.

We arrived two hours before our meeting. I decided to take Gully along since he knew where the location was, and also in case I needed back up. We were parked in a van about a block away from the address we had given to Agent Joseph. We wanted to make sure he came alone. Forty-five minutes went by when we noticed a black Ford Taurus pull up to the location.

"Is that him?" Gully asked anxiously.

"We're about to find out now," I responded.

We watched a man get out of his car and walk to the front of the building. He looked around, taking in his surroundings, then he walked around the whole building before returning to his car.

"Bingo, that's him," I said, nodding.

We watched him for the next thirty minutes in order to make sure he was alone. We noticed a few cars slow down, but nothing suspicious. Before I got out of the van, I grabbed my gun, just in case my instincts were wrong. I exited the van and walked toward his car. I went to the passenger side and knocked on his window. He unlocked the door, and I opened it and sat down. We stared at each other for what seemed like thirty minutes.

"Da-David!" Agent Joseph said, astonished. I was the last person he expected to see.

54

Agent Joseph

Chico owned a mini-mansion in Central Islip, Long Island. It was secluded in a wooded area and had eight bedrooms, five bathrooms, an indoor pool, and even a basketball court. According to the blueprints, the house contained twelve hidden passageways. Several of them led to various exits throughout different parts of the house, and two served as hideouts. There was good reason to believe that Jerry aka King was hidden in one of these rooms.

Agent Joseph spread the word around the neighborhood where he believed some of the Body Snatchers frequented that Major was being held captive in Chico's house and included the address.

Agent Joseph's team had had the house under surveillance for the past week, hoping to see some kind of movement that would help lead them to the rescue of Jerry. This location was good for people who needed to be totally isolated. There homes had a great deal of distance between them. The roads were dark and narrow, with trees surrounding the entire area. The little light that shone was emitted from the post lights that were located on Chico's property. It appeared that no one was home, but the team knew there were always men standing on guard nearby. That kind of security was not out of the ordinary for a political consultant. Currently, Agent Joseph's team was stationed in a three-story abandoned structure, positioned about a hundred yards north of Chico's property. All the trees surrounding it made it almost impossible to have a clear view of the property. They settled in on the upper level because it had an overhead view. Agent Joseph was just starting to relax and placed his binoculars down when suddenly something caught his attention. He spotted rapid movement on Chico's property.

"Holy shit!" he said, nearly falling off his seat.

It was like something out of a movie. He adjusted the focus on his binoculars and zoomed in. Agent Joseph had twelve agents in the building with him, but there were at least thirty men running onto Chico's property.

"What is it?" Agent Camper asked, coming to stand beside Agent Joseph who gave him the binoculars for him to check it out for himself. Although Agent Camper was still suspended, Agent Joseph allowed Agent Camper to tag along since he was so integral to the mission. However, he told Agent Camper earlier that he was not to intervene. Instead he ordered him to stand down.

Agent Joseph started barking orders for his team to assemble.

"Oh shit!" Agent Camper yelled.

"Listen, everyone! Saddle up! We're going to break up into teams. Agent Wright, you take the five men on the left and go around the back. Agent Jones will take the remaining five and go around the front. I'm going to need everyone to stay as close as possible to each other. Alright, let's move out!" Agent Joseph ordered, checking the safety latch on his gun.

55

David

After meeting with Agent Joseph, everything fell right into place. We received information regarding the location of my brother and also where Chico was staying. We were heading out there tonight to get Jerry and to deal with Chico. My instincts were right. Agent Joseph and I did have a connection. He is my uncle. We knew of him because he visited us a few times when we were younger. Over the years he lost touch with us, but our mother always talked about him and how well he was doing in America. It was a bittersweet reunion. I explained to him what went down in Haiti and that Chico was responsible for murdering my family. I also told him Chico held a grudge he wanted to settle with us, and that's why he kidnapped Jerry. Agent Joseph already knew about Jerry's kidnapping from his partner, Agent Camper. We talked about what our next steps should be and formulated a plan to get Jerry back and us out of town.

Dressed in black, my squad and I moved quickly through the woods. Ricky and his team covered the opposite side of the house. I scanned the backyard of the house and didn't see anyone. The tension was thick in the air. I crouched low and gestured for my team to follow me.

Suddenly, I stopped. Something didn't feel right. I turned to check if everyone was still in position, when a shot was fired.

I saw one of my boy's head whip backwards from the strength of the bullet entering his forehead. Everyone started letting off shots toward the house.

I ran for cover and ducked behind a parked car near the garage.

"Yo, Major!" Jinx said dropping next to me. "You ain't hit, right?" He looked at my vest.

"Nah, I'm good. I'm gonna need you to cover me while I make a run for the garage door," I said quickly.

"No problem," he replied.

My heart was beating a million miles per second, and my adrenaline was running high.

Jinx stood up, leaned over the hood of the car, and let his shotgun ring.

He loved that shotgun. That's all he ever talked about, ever since he had the chance to shoot that agent in the face. I stood up and took off, keeping my head low, and ran for the garage door.

56

Agent Joseph

Observing the area, Agent Joseph instantly dropped low to the ground. Bodies were dropping and bullets were flying in every direction. He heard a crash and looked up at the house. A body went flying out of the window, and landed on top of a car setting off the alarm.

"I'm going in!" Agent Joseph said, through his earpiece.

He heard a noise first then saw movement from the corner of his eye. An arm swung down on him in a chopping motion, causing him to fall to his knees. Agent Joseph quickly rolled over and fired his weapon. The perp grabbed his neck and stumbled to the ground. Gunshots began to hail like a storm, taking the perp out of his misery.

Agent Joseph saw an open door near the garage. He stood and ran inside. It was dark, so he knew he had to be extremely careful. Remembering the blueprints, he knew one of the hideouts was located in the basement. There was a passageway through the dining room on the first floor that should lead him to his destination. The dining room was massive and contained huge bay windows. A long, neatly arranged dining table sat in the center of the room with fine china and silverware neatly placed side by side.

Approaching the antique grandfather clock, he searched for the latch to open the cover of the case. He pulled down on the swinging handle and heard movement behind him. Heading to the other side of the room, a statue of the Virgin Mary glided to the left. Stepping inside the passageway, he made his way down the spiral steps. Agent Joseph pushed open a door and stepped into a room.

Although seemingly empty, the basement was spacious. Black pipes lined the ceilings of the gray painted walls. Against one wall, an oil lamp stood on top of a wooden table. In the center of the dimly lit room there was a chair occupied by a young woman, rocking something in her arms and a little girl stood in the far corner.

"Hey, are you alright?" Agent Joseph whispered, moving toward the individual. "My name is Agent Joseph, and I'm with the FBI."

Without warning he heard the unmistakable sound of a gun click.

"I want you to lay your gun down and lock your fingers behind your head," the voice commanded.

"Fifi, pick up the gun, and if he moves, shoot him," the male voice said.

The woman followed his instructions.

"What are we gonna do now, Jerry?" she asked, staring behind me.

Agent Joseph's back stiffened as he felt hands patting his waist, looking for a concealed weapon.

"How have you been, J.J.?" Agent Joseph asked, feeling the hands stop. Agent Joseph relaxed and bore a smile.

"Turn around," he commanded.

J.J. was a nickname Agent Joseph had given Jerry when he was a little boy. When Agent Joseph turned around, his heart sank.

"Uncle Jamie?" Jerry grimaced.

Jerry's face and lips were swollen and bruised. It was apparent he had been beaten severely while being held captive. Some of the bruises were old and looked like they were healing while others look like fresh cuts and wounds.

The last time Agent Joseph saw the twins together was at the funeral for their father, Reginald, many moons ago. At the time he made a vow to his dead brother to look after and care for his family, but Agent Joseph fell short on his word and had failed his brother and the family miserably. Instead, he became self-absorbed with his career. He obtained his degree, went through the ranks to became a federal agent and never looked back. His sister-in-law Barbara, niece and nephew Johnny were dead, and every law enforcement agency in America was searching for David and Jerry. However, Agent Joseph felt he owed it to his family and couldn't let them find the twins. After he and David hooked up they came up with a plan, and part of that plan was to rescue Jerry.

"What are you doing here?" he asked.

"Listen, we have to get you out of here. We don't have much time. I have a van waiting for all of you out back. We have to leave now," Agent Joseph said, handing him his bullet proof vest. "I'll lead the way. I want them behind me," he said, referring to Fifi, the baby, and the little girl. "Jerry, you cover the back."

As they headed out of the basement, they didn't know what awaited them next.

57

David

I looked at my watch and cursed. We were running out of time. Gunfire and sirens filled the air, and in the dark it was hard to see who was winning the battle. The house seemed to become darker, the deeper I went inside. My senses were on overdrive. I hoped Uncle Jamie had gotten Jerry out. Uncle Jamie tried to change my mind about coming tonight, but I was not going to let Chico get away from me that easily. I looked at my watch again. Ten minutes remaining.

The corridor was long, and picture frames and plaques covered both walls. As I crept down the walkway, I stopped at a door. I reached for the doorknob and pushed. It was nothing but a bathroom. Moving farther down the hall, I pushed opened another door and saw it was only a bedroom. *Where the hell was this bastard hiding?* I asked myself. Suddenly, I saw movement, but I was a little too late. A blow came colliding into my jaw, and I felt something snap. *That's going to hurt later,* I thought. Falling against the wall, I tried to regain my balance. Again, I was either a little too late or he was just fast as hell as I felt another punch smash against my face. Immediately, I felt my eye and saw that big star that people say they see when they get punched really hard.

"You piece of shit! You thought you could kill my son and get away with it!" Chico shouted as I lay down on the floor.

I tried to regain my focus, but couldn't. My vision was blurred, and I was trying to reach for my gun.

"I'm going to make sure I murder that pretty aunt of yours myself!" he said, kicking me in the stomach. Regaining my vision, his image became clearer. Outside of the weight loss, and despite wearing a full-grown beard, he looked the same. I saw him reach for my Tek on the floor.

"Don't worry. Your brother will be with you very soon. Say hello to your mother for me," he said, cocking the gun.

I threw my hands up to guard my face and waited for the inevitable. Then, I heard a piercing sound.

I looked up and saw Chico fall to his knees with his eyes rolling in the back of his head. Behind him stood Ricky my Haitian4Life, wearing a satisfied look on his face. Kicking Chico's limp body to the floor, Ricky stepped on his back and pulled the machete out.

"Faggot," Ricky said, spitting on him.

"What took you so long?" I asked, rising from the floor.

He shrugged.

"Come on! They're waiting for us downstairs," he said.

Retrieving my Tek off the floor, I smiled and lead the way. "We out."

Ricky looked down at Chico's body lying on the floor and said, "It felt good chopping that nigga in the back. Now, I can move on with my life. When you told me about some dude named Chico and what he did to your family, I knew it couldn't be a coincidence. That punk ass hurt a lot of people, including my family. For a long time, I'd been waiting and dreaming about this moment. I just couldn't wait to get my hands on that nigga."

"Where's everybody?" I asked, surprised at Ricky's testimony.

"In the car, but yo, that nigga was fucking your ass up," Ricky said, laughing.

"Fuck you, nigga," I said, chuckling.

Just ahead, two men jumped out from around the corner with guns aimed at us.

"Freeze! Police!" one man shouted.

"Move!" I yelled, raising my Tek.

Standing beside Ricky, I bumped him hard on his shoulder, pushing him into the bedroom. Gunshots blasted at us from down the hallway.

"Major!" I heard Ricky shout.

As quickly as it started, the gunshots suddenly stopped. Ricky got up and pointed his gun in the direction where he last saw the cops. Everyone was lying on the ground. He looked over and saw me lying on my back with my eyes open, staring up at the ceiling. Tears were streaming down my face. The impact of the bullets came unexpectedly and felt like someone had lit me on fire with a torch. My body felt both hot and cold as I felt my insides burning, but my teeth chattered. He knelt down beside me and asked, "What the fuck you do that for?"

He ripped my shirt open and saw bullets lodged in my vest. It wasn't until he saw the blood flowing from my neck, that his expression changed and I knew it was over for me. We heard walkie-talkies in the distance and footsteps rapidly approaching.

"I got you, my nigga," Ricky said, making a promise to me. "Haitians4Life!" he said and gripped my hand firmly before he left.

"Haitians4Life!" I murmured.

Ricky picked up his gun and ran back to the bedroom, locking the door behind him. He ran to the walk-in closet, straight to a full-length mirror that was placed on the floor. He pushed on the glass and backed away. The mirror spun 180 degrees, like a revolving door. Ricky ran down the passageway. Seconds later, he heard the crash of the bedroom door. Turning the corner, he ran down the long flight of stairs that led to the ground floor.

I watched as Ricky made his escape through the bedroom and listened to walkie-talkies as they grew closer. My eyelids became heavy, and I finally succumbed and watched my life flash before me. Images of my family, friends, and even enemies ran through my mind. Knowing my brother was safe and that bastard Chico was dead gave me great satisfaction. My only regret was not seeing my brother before leaving this earth. I knew Aunt Kathy and Lauren would be around to hold him down. I closed my eyes and thought about the good old days back in Haiti.

My last thought was, *Haitians4Life*.

58

Agent Joseph

Agent Joseph, David, Fifi, the baby, and the little girl were walking through Chico's mansion, and gunfire along with sounds of agony continued to invade the space. Agent Joseph was leading them to safety. He explained to Jerry that David got in contact with him and described how they devised a plan to get him out of there.

"Where is David?" Jerry asked.

"He's upstairs looking for Chico. I told him the FBI would handle him, but he insisted on dealing with him one-on-one," Agent Joseph said.

"Who are they?" Agent Joseph asked, pointing to the young lady, the baby, and the little girl.

"That's Fifi, Chico's niece; that's my baby, Barbara; and my little sister, Loria," Jerry said, pointing to each individual.

"Who? I thought Chico killed the remaining family?" Agent Joseph asked, shocked.

"I saved her and took her to my house," Fifi responded.

Agent Joseph paused for a moment and looked at Loria. He was amazed at how much she resembled her mother. Agent Joseph touched Fifi on her shoulder and said, "Thank you."

They proceeded walking through Chico's mansion, finally reaching the back of the house. Agent Joseph opened the back door and saw the van outside waiting for them. Everyone ran to the van, and Jerry and the others climbed into the back. Agent Joseph walked to the front of the van, gave the driver the rest of the money owed, and instructed him to wait for two more people. Agent Joseph briskly headed back into the house and waited for David.

Closing the back door, Agent Joseph spied one of Chico's men as he tried to blindside him. He charged Agent Joseph from behind, knocking him to the floor. Agent Joseph flipped over and swung his foot, hitting the attacker behind his knees. The move caused the man to lose his balance, and he banged his head on the edge of a shelf. The attacker was unconscious. Agent Joseph heard more movements and ran behind the door so he could ambush whoever was coming down the stairwell. Seconds later, he saw Ricky running toward the door, but he was alone.

"Ricky!" Agent Joseph shouted.

He stopped at hearing his name.

"Where's David?" Agent Joseph asked.

He shook his head and gave him a sad blank look.

"He's gone. Those fucking pigs shot him, and they're working their way through the house now!"

Dropping to the ground, he placed his face into my hands and muffled a scream. He did manage to tell Ricky to go and not to look back.

Agent Joseph could hear the cries from Jerry as the van made its escape. He figured something was wrong when he didn't see David. Agent Joseph beat himself up for not being firmer with David. He should have said or done something to deter David from coming along. Once again he held himself responsible for David's death. He felt life wasn't giving him a fair hand.

The door swung open, and police bombarded the space.

"Don't move! Drop your weapons and raise your hands!" an officer commanded.

The squad had their guns drawn.

"It's alright. I'm with the FBI," Agent Joseph said, waving them off.

"Drop your weapon, now!" he repeated.

Agent Joseph complied. Agent Camper walked out from behind a policeman.

"Camper, tell them everything is alright," Agent Joseph requested.

"You're a disgrace to the department," Agent Camper said, walking toward him.

Agent Joseph frowned, wondering why Agent Camper suddenly turned on him.

"What are you talking about? Stop playing and make them holster their guns," Agent Joseph said still playing innocent and keeping his anger in check.

"What? You thought you would get away with this? You should have jumped in that van with them," Agent Camper said, snatching Agent Joseph's earpiece off his shirt.

Aww fuck! Agent Joseph thought.

Agent Joseph thought getting caught was a possibility, but he didn't mean to be so sloppy. He was a professional and went into this job with a clouded mind and poor judgment, but he knew he had to do this final deed for his family, especially after failing his brother and now himself. Agent Joseph's final wish now was that Jerry would take care of himself.

"Uncle Jamie, you are under arrest for aiding and abetting a fug—" Agent Camper said before Agent Joseph snatched his gun off his hip. Agent Joseph's last memory was the look of terror in Agent Camper's eyes.

59

Agent Camper

Agent Camper was still inside of the stake-out house, observing the action as it took place on Chico's property. He saw shadows and figures moving rapidly and sparks resembling fireworks. He didn't feel Agent Joseph had recruited enough men for this mission. Agent Camper tried making a call on the land line for additional backup, but the line was dead. Then, he recalled leaving his cell phone in the car. Once outside, the gunfire sounded even more like the wild, wild west. "We definitely needed more man power," he said.

Agent Camper hurried through the front yard to where the car was parked. When he arrived at the car, he couldn't find the phone in the armrest. After a more detailed search he found it in the middle console. Attempting to call in the cavalry, he realized this phone had no signal either.

"Fuck," he yelled, punching the dashboard.

Thinking quickly, he remembered Agent Wright had a two-way radio in his car. He would use that to call the local police and get additional manpower. Agent Camper darted out of his car and ran to Agent Wright's vehicle. Once he yanked the door open, a light automatically turned on, and there it was, like a beam shining down from the heavens. Hastily, Agent Camper called the operator and asked to be patched in to the local police department. He informed the chief that a shootout was taking place in his town, and that he might want to get some men out there, pronto. The chief was outraged that something like this was happening in his district and he wasn't even aware of it. He promised to have at least twenty men sent out within the next twenty minutes. Agent Camper placed the radio down and breathed a sigh of relief, pleased that backup would be arriving shortly.

Agent Camper waited in the car for the backup to arrive. He placed the earpiece back into his ear so he could hear what was taking place on the property. Initially the only sounds to be heard after the gunfire died down was a lot of foot movement. After five minutes of silence, he heard Agent Joseph talking to someone in another language that sounded like French. They easily switched from English to Creole. Agent Camper was shocked after hearing the other person refer to him as Uncle Jamie. *Did I hear correctly? Uncle Jamie?* Agent Camper wondered and continued listening. Could it be possible that Agent Joseph was aiding and abetting members of the Body Snatchers? He simply couldn't believe this could be true.

Agent Camper grew furious over what he heard. Agent Joseph was talking about making arrangements for their getaway. Did Agent Joseph set up this entire stakeout? he wondered. Agent Camper looked down at his watch and noticed fifteen minutes had passed. *Where the hell are they?* he thought. Time is wasting. Five minutes later, he saw headlights off in the distance. Finally, he thought. He got out of the car and waved to get their attention. When they gathered, he briefed the men on what to expect, then made his way toward the house, hoping to find Agent Joseph and the twins to take them in.

Agent Camper and the officers ran onto Chico's property. He had the men separate into teams. He took seven men with him to find Agent Joseph. Agent Camper figured Agent Joseph's nephews would be with him, too, and therefore would need the extra help. One of the men kicked the door open leading to the garage where they discovered Agent Joseph. Agent Camper approached him, and said, "Uncle Jamie, you are under arrest for aiding and abetting a fugitive."

The men spread throughout the room with their guns aimed. Agent Joseph was caught off guard. He looked surprised to hear him say Uncle Jamie. He grabbed Agent Camper's gun and pointed it at him. They struggled as he tried to get him to put down the gun. Agent Camper knew the officers would not hesitate to shoot Agent Joseph who cocked the gun and mumbled something in Creole. The officers immediately opened fire, riddling his body with bullets. Agent Camper screamed, "No!" He knew killing him was the easy way out. Now they'd never learn the full details and answers to questions they had about the case. Agent Camper watched as Agent Joseph's body crumpled to the floor, and he cursed him. They came and left with nothing but more casualties. Agent Camper walked out, feeling defeated once again.

Two days later...

Agent Camper walked into his office and stood behind his desk. He plopped down into a chair and took a deep breath. He pulled out the file on the Body Snatchers case to review for any missing clues or links. Agent Camper reclined in his chair and reflected over the events of the past couple of months. Who would have thought that Agent Joseph was an accomplice to the twins? After all, he was their uncle. How deeply involved was he? Agent Camper wondered.

These guys just wouldn't quit, not even after the death of one of their leaders. Now they had kidnapped Director Savelli, the head of the FBI. They were blaming him for the death of David Benton aka Major, saying he was the one who orchestrated the plan to capture the Body Snatchers, and he should be held responsible. This time, they left a note but didn't ask for a ransom. Agent Camper's gut feeling told him Director Savelli was already a dead man. Looking at his watch, he thought about the briefing he had to give within the next fifteen minutes to a new team that was now working on the case.

He got up from his desk and walked to the window that overlooked the parking lot. He caught a quick glimpse of his reflection in the window and almost didn't recognize himself. Since taking on this case, he had lost ten pounds, countless hours of sleep, and hadn't shaved in days. Agent Camper knew he was in dire need of a bona fide vacation real soon. Maybe even a permanent one once the dust settled and this case was closed. After studying himself further, he simply shook his head in disgust and proceeded out the door for the briefing.

As soon as Agent Camper entered the room, he got straight to business. Flipping through the slides, he gave the group a breakdown of the events as they had occurred thus far. When he was done, he turned off the projector and flipped on the light switch.

"As you know, these men call themselves the Body Snatchers, and they are relentless. Ladies and gentlemen, these men have captured Director Savelli, and honestly, I don't think there is a chance of getting him back alive, but we must stop at nothing as we give this our all. We are dealing with methodical and intelligent serial killers. They have the resources and financing to inflict extreme harm to our citizens," he said to his captive audience of agents.

"Are there any photographs of these suspects we can use?" asked one of the agents.

"Yes," Agent Camper replied, turning to his file folder. He took out the pictures and handed them to him.

"Make copies of those photographs and memorize those faces," he said, glancing at each agent. "I have a gut feeling these faces are about to become our never-ending nightmare."

60

Agent Camper

I'm telling you, this isn't going to work," Agent Camper said.

"Why not? It's perfect. We bring her in, put the word out, and we'll wait," Agent Rodriguez simply stated.

This entire plan is wrong, Camper thought. The plan just didn't feel right to him. The new FBI director, Smith, wanted Jerry's mother arrested. The bureau decided it would be best if the twins' mother was brought in to custody first because it would eventually lead the fugitive into captivity.

The plan was to bring the mother in under obstruction of justice charges, then bargain for her release for the arrest of her son. Truth be told, everyone was starting to get desperate. The citizens of New York were now demanding answers. The governor was under a lot of close scrutiny because foreign figures were now making public statements about the situation. The media and press were taking the story and running with it, and having a field day. But the investigation on the Body Snatchers seemed to be leading nowhere. No one was talking out of fear of being the next one on the Body Snatchers' list to be killed.

Agent Camper just had a bad feeling about this. They were dealing with a bunch of young adults with resources and the mind capacity of radicals.

"This is kidnapping, and it's totally wrong," Agent Camper stated as he stepped out of his vehicle.

"Desperate times call for desperate measures," Agent Rodriguez replied and followed Agent Camper to the house door.

Agent Camper shook his head in disbelief.

Agent Rodriguez was a short, stout man who was new in the field. He was your average gung-ho federal rookie. He wanted to dive in head first into the case and make an arrest. Director Smith assigned Agents Camper and Rodriguez as partners. Agent Camper thought it was a bad idea to assign a virgin to this complicated case.

"He's not ready for a case on this level," Agent Camper pleaded to the director, but it fell on deaf ears.

The director felt it was indeed the right decision, and that this case could use some new blood and different outlook.

"It will show a lesson and prove to him that this life demands more brains than balls," he retorted.

But Agent Camper knew differently.

When he rang the doorbell, a shadow appeared from behind the blinds. The door swung open, and Jerry's sister, Lauren, answered. Agent Camper ignored her attitude.

"Yes!" she said, seething.

Agent Camper had been through this many times, and every time, it was the same scenario. "I am Agent Camper, and this is Agent Rodriguez," he said, reintroducing himself. "We would like to speak to your mother, Ms. Katherine Benton."

"For what? Y'all have been here like a hundred times already, and you leave with the same information y'all came with—nothing. We don't know anything! How many times aré we going to tell you that?" Lauren stated, twisting her head to the side.

"Listen, ma'am, we're with the FBI, okay? So, go get Ms. Benton out here, now!" Agent Rodriguez erupted.

"Hold up! You are not—" Lauren was interrupted.

"Lauren, it's alright. How can I help you?" Aunt Kathy said, stepping out onto the porch.

"Ms. Benton, can you please come with us. We have a warrant for your arrest," Agent Rodriguez stated.

"Arrest?" she gasped, placing her hand over her chest.

"Arrest! You must be outta your mind!" Lauren yelled, stepping in front of her mother. "For what? You're not taking my mother anywhere!" She stretched her arms out in order to shield her mother.

"Ma'am, can you please step aside?" Agent Camper asked, as he took out a pair of handcuffs.

Aunt Kathy was so overwhelmed that she couldn't speak. She couldn't understand why she was being arrested. As far as she was concerned, she hadn't done anything wrong or illegal. She knew she was being followed, so she had been very cautious. She did not want to believe it was her nephews who were responsible for the all the turmoil going on, but when Jerry told her about the death of David, reality hit her. She wanted to blame herself for what was happening. She should have been stricter with her nephews, giving them guidelines and rules to follow.

"My mother," Lauren said, placing emphasis on *mother*, "is not going anywhere."

Before Agent Camper could respond, Agent Rodriguez stepped forward and grabbed Lauren's arm.

"Get your damn hand off me!" Lauren said, swinging wildly.

Agent Rodriguez seized Lauren by the arms and pushed her, face first, into the wall.

You're hurting me! Let me go!" she bawled.

Aunt Kathy snapped out of her momentary shock and jumped on Agent Rodriguez.

Agent Camper restrained her and placed the cuffs onto her wrists.

"Ms. Benton, you are under arrest for obstruction of justice."

61

Jerry

King, just the man I wanted to see."

Frank Lucci also known as Frankie "the Bull" Lucci was the reputed head boss of the Lucci crime family. He was called the Bull for apparent reasons. He stood at six-three, had a gigantic physique, and a round face that made him look like a power lifter. Frankie's toothpick mustache and smooth skin concealed his true age of forty-five. He wore a grin that won over the hearts of the deadliest men in the street. Frank was very wise and street smart. He was known as the con man with the flaring temper in his family. However, his one shortcoming was his tantrums, which had caused the family embarrassment and unwanted attention on numerous occasions. The family tolerated him due to his status as a Capo, his ability to finesse and get deals done, and because his father was Giovanni Lucci.

Frankie was no one's fool. He knew all about the secret meetings that were held in his name behind his back. He felt the insincere handshakes and caught some unpleasant stares from his peers. He even had information on the man standing in front of him. When he first heard of the Body Snatchers, he was amused to know they were the ones responsible for the murder of the governor's son.

Those arrogant fucks, Frankie thought.

Frankie respected the reputation the Body Snatchers earned and was shocked to hear they were just a bunch of young guys who were the masterminds behind the entire operation. To think a bunch of kids were responsible for all this mayhem was truly incredible.

Frankie admired King's courage and had a considerable amount of respect for him. When Frankie got wind King was looking to buy weapons, he immediately sent his lieutenant Joey Sticks to put the word out he wanted to talk to him. That was several months ago. It took a while for Frankie and his people to get word to them because the Haitian community was so tight lipped about having strangers ask too many questions.

Frankie owned a restaurant and bar called Echoes, located in the lower east side of Manhattan, near Canal Street. A lot of tourists and business moguls frequented his restaurant. Echoes was one of the go-to spots in New York City, known for its delicious food and high-quality service. In order to get a table, you had to make a reservation at least six months in advance. Since the restaurant was so popular, Frankie had security on staff around the clock.

There was one table that was off limits and must never be requested. Booth 7 was Frankie Lucci's exclusive table. One day, Frankie arrived, only to discover a red-and-blue envelope placed on top of his seat. After reading the note, Frankie demanded to know how the letter got there. No one could give him an explanation, not even the security staff. Frankie then fired and replaced his entire security staff.

Lucky was the head of security and a full-blooded Sicilian. He was almost fired along with the previous security staff but was spared, only because Joey Sticks had put in a good word for him. After that episode, Lucky held a deep grudge against King.

"King and his band of monkeys," he would call them.

On more than one occasion, Lucky had to be reprimanded for his behavior toward King.

Frankie said, "If King can penetrate our already tight-knit security, then King is to be respected because men like that will always keep you on your toes."

In the same breath he would also say, "Don't fuck with that man. He is not your average Moulignon or Moulie."

But Lucky thought otherwise. To him, all blacks were low-down, dirty moulies and didn't deserve respect. They were lower than the scum on the bottom of his shoes. Since King infiltrated his security, it showed the lack of respect he had for him and his team, and he didn't like being disrespected.

Lucky stood behind Frankie and eavesdropped on the conversation.

"Have a seat," Frankie offered. "My place is your place."

"Thank you," King said, taking a seat beside Frankie so that he could watch the entrance of the restaurant.

"Get this man a drink," Frankie ordered the waitress.

"No, I'm alright. I just want to get down to business," King said.

Frankie just nodded. "Something bothering you?" he asked.

King remained silent. "I need a favor," he finally said.

"What is it? Is something wrong?" Frank asked, leaning forward.

Frankie took everything King said seriously. King was not known for playing games and joking around. There were times Frankie felt King should loosen up around the edges a little. Frankie dealt with some of the world's most cold-blooded killers. There was nothing fake about King. People might have mistaken him as just another harmless kid, but not Frankie. When he looked into his eyes, he could tell he hadn't led the life of an average kid. He knew those eyes—steel gray like a tempest rising, unbreakable, unwavering eyes—had stories to tell.

Frankie sensed deep down something was bothering him, and it was slowly starting to eat away at him. He'd seen it happen many times before, a man with one too many problems carrying the weight of the world on his shoulders, turning into a ticking bomb.

"Is there something I can do?"

Since Frankie was from the streets, he knew having a man like King in his debt could only benefit him.

"You know, I have a lot of respect for you, Frankie."

"Thank you. My family and I feel the same way about you."

Lucky huffed and gave a little chuckle. The laugh was a betrayal to Frankie's statement.

"Is there something funny?" Frankie growled to Lucky.

"No, Frankie," Lucky said, catching himself.

"Then why the fuck are you's laughing?" Frankie yelled. "Get the fuck outta here!" He pointed to the door.

They waited for Lucky to leave before they spoke again.

"Sorry about that," Frankie offered.

King nodded. "Listen, I like doing business with you, Frank, and I would like for it to continue."

"So would I, but what is this about?"

"I need you to keep doing business with my people, even if I'm not here," King said, staring at Frankie.

Frankie understood very well and nodded.

"You're alright with me," Frankie said, letting King know he had his back.

King's phone rang, and he excused himself so that he could answer it. Once King stepped away, whoever was on the line caused him to yell a string of obscenities and kick over one of the tables.

62

Jerry

Everyone in the restaurant stopped what they were doing and the place fell quiet as they watched the commotion going down. I was enraged over the phone call and screamed into the phone, cursing everything alive, and I felt like I was having some sort of out-of-body experience. That's when I saw Lucky walk back into the restaurant to find out what all the noise was about.

"King, calm down, and tell me what's going on. You're drawing too much attention to us," Frankie said.

I smashed my phone down to the ground, breaking it into several pieces.

Lucky moved to grab me, but Frankie held his hand up to stop him. Instead, he ordered Lucky to go around and assure everyone that things were under control.

"King, what's going on?" Frankie whispered.

I stared at Frankie, knowing my eyes were red with anger.

"They took my mother, Frankie," I said.

"Who? Who took your mother?" Frankie asked, frowning.

"The feds."

"Oh boy," Frankie said. "The feds? For what?"

"I don't know yet, but they're trying to use her to get to me. Those fucking bastards."

"Tell me what happened," Frankie said, trying to make sense of everything.

"I just know that the feds went to my house and arrested my mother and that my sister was there and raised hell. One of those motherfuckers put his hands on her," I said, taking a deep breath.

"They're dead, Frankie. I'm tired of this shit," I said with determination and finality.

Frankie nodded. "I know if the shoe was on the other foot, I would be saying the same thing. I understand how you're feeling, King," Frankie said. "But are you sure you want to do that? That's a whole new ball game." Frankie lit up his cigar.

I glared at him in silence. He didn't know me very well. He may have heard things, but he hadn't even scratched the surface.

"Okay," Frankie said. "Listen, King, I can understand how you feel, but you have to understand the position I'm in. I can't get involved in this situation or drag my whole family into this, but I'm not going to let you leave here empty-handed."

I was in another world, beginning to draft a plan. "Alright, Frankie."

Blowing a cloud of smoke into the air, Frankie continued, "Like I said, I'm not going to let you leave here empty-handed. I may have some tools that might be of some interest to you.

63

Jerry

Somewhere in the basement of an abandoned building in Brownsville, shots were being echoed off the surrounding walls. Wearing earmuffs, Jinx was practicing his long-distance shooting. Gully was nearby, standing behind Meena, teaching her how to fire a handgun properly. Britney was sitting next to Bones, bopping her head to the music that was playing on the radio. She was passing the blunt to Ricky and being entertained by Fifi and Mrs. Kelly who were arguing for the hundredth time.

The tension between Mrs. Kelly and Fifi had been building ever since their first encounter. When Mrs. Kelly first met Fifi, she figured she was a person of interest and wanted to know more about her relationship with Jerry. After snooping around, she heard the shorter version of what happened back in Haiti. She found out that Fifi was originally David's girlfriend but had a baby with Jerry. Once she heard that, her hatred toward Fifi grew more and more with each passing day. She blamed her for the kidnapping and for David's death. Fifi, on the other hand, didn't like Mrs. Kelly because she thought she was an old hag who was trying to recapture her youth. She saw how she was fawning all over Jerry, and by the way she looked at him, she could tell this was more than just a friendship. Fifi also felt she couldn't be trusted ever since she overheard Mrs. Kelly was the one who told the cops Jerry had been kidnapped. When she voiced her concerns to Jerry, he brushed her suggestions off as ludicrous.

"Both of y'all need to cut this shit out," Ricky's girlfriend Geneva said, placing the Glock on the table.

"If she keeps running her mouth, I'm gonna have to show her who this little girl is," Fifi said, pointing her finger at Mrs. Kelly.

"Little girl, I don't know what you take me for, but trust me when I say I'll rearrange all that furniture in your mouth. I mean it!" Mrs. Kelly threatened and stepped forward.

Britney was high as hell and just burst out laughing as they continued to bicker.

"Both y'all bitches need to sit your asses down 'cause ain't none of you about to do anything," Britney said.

"Who the fuck is you?" Fifi demanded.

Ricky grimaced and decided to end the quarreling before blows were exchanged.

"Everyone needs to calm down! This is not the right time to be fighting. All of us here love King. He needs our help right now, and if y'all love him like y'all say y'all do, then you should be worrying about helping him," Ricky stated, calming the women down.

A door slammed, and King walked through, dragging a box.

Ricky ran over to get the box.

"Oh, baby!" Ricky exclaimed, opening the box flaps.

"There's more upstairs," King said, placing a stack of newspapers on the table.

"This is it, right here," he said, pointing at an article. "For those of you who stuck with me from the very beginning, when David and I first came to y'all with our ideas and plans, y'all know what to expect. This is where the men are separated from the boys and the women from the girls. For those who joined us later, you are now members of the Body Snatchers. For the past year, we've been preparing ourselves for a day like this. Everyone here should be well experienced and ready for any situation. That's why we ran drills all month so we were prepared for this occasion," he said, then paused.

"Them motherfuckers done killed my brother and thought they had the upper hand. Now they have my mother in some jail, and they put their grimy hands on my sister. Somebody's gonna pay. There's no turning back now."

"Women cannot become Body Snatchers. Today is the birthday of Pretty Posse, our female extension. Sharon and Fifi will not be involved in this scheme. They will be in charge of communications, financing, and artillery."

"What the hell is this?" Ricky asked, holding up a black-colored device.

"That's a location scrambler. We'll get to that a little later," King explained. "Right now, we're going to make a few calls and put some things in order. Y'all with me?" King glanced around.

"Haitians4Life," the men said in unison.

King smiled and read the front page of the newspaper with the headline, MOTHER-SNATCHERS ARRESTED!

"I hope they are all ready to die!" King said as he laid out his latest gun acquisitions.

64

FBI Headquarters

What that hell was that?" Director Smith yelled.

"She was interfering with an arrest," Agent Rodriguez pleaded.

Agent Camper was still amazed at Agent Rodriguez's actions. All they had to do was get to Queens, pick up the mother, and bring her downtown. This was supposed to be an easy assignment, and Agent Rodriguez managed to make a circus out of it. Now they were sitting with their fingers crossed, hoping the papers only got wind of the arrest and not the entire altercation.

Agent Camper knew Ms. Benton had no involvement or knowledge of what her kids were up to. The bureau had her phone tapped, and none of her conversations indicated anything out of the ordinary. *What else could possibly go wrong?* Agent Camper thought.

The phone rang.

Director Smith answered. "Smith," he said into the speakerphone.

"Turn on the television," the caller ordered.

"Who is this?" the director quizzed. "Senator Williams, turn on your TV—now!"

The director nodded to Agent Camper, and he turned on the TV and increased the volume.

"This just in: We have confirmed a report that the Body Snatchers have just declared war against all police officials!" the reporter said. "A confidential source stated that the FBI wrongly detained the mother of alleged Body Snatcher Jerry Benton. The Body Snatchers are claiming the bureau also allegedly assaulted the sister of Mr. Benton while in the process of arresting the mother. It is reported that Mr. Benton became infuriated when he heard this and has declared war until Katherine Benton is released. More on this story, after the break," the reporter said.

Agent Camper shut the TV off.

"Now, please tell me, director, what in the world is going on?" the senator barked.

Director Smith looked as if he was about to explode.

"Sen—" Director Smith said before getting cut off.

"You have a call on line two," said the receptionist, barging into the room.

"Can't you see I'm in a meeting?" growled the director.

"The caller demanded to speak with you, sir," she replied nervously.

The director sighed.

"Excuse me, senator. I have an urgent call I have to take." He switched lines. "Smith!"

"For each day my mother is in your custody, a cop will die, and every day after that, the number will increase," the caller threatened.

"Who is this?" Director Smith asked, stalling for time as he waved wildly for Agent Camper to trace the call.

Agent Camper ran out of the office and into another room.

"No time for games. Your men will die if my mother is not released."

"We apologize for the assault on your sister, Jerry," Director Smith said. "We'd be glad to release your mother if you would turn yourself in. What do you say?"

"I say fuck you! How about that?" the voice replied, then he hung up.

"Hello. Hello? Fuck!" Director Smith shouted.

"The address is 250-102 89th Road, Apartment L1," Agent Camper shouted, rushing back into the office.

"What are you waiting for, Christmas? Get down there, now!" Director Smith yelled.

65

Agent Camper

Agent Camper had thirty-five agents surround the ten-story apartment building in Queens. Twelve agents stood in the lobby of the spacious building, ready to go upstairs and break down the door of apartment L1. Agent Crown, captain of Team Alpha, waited ahead of his men for further instructions from Agent Camper.

Meanwhile, two blocks away on the rooftop of a building, King watched the escapade unfold through military-style binoculars. Nearby, Ricky sat smoking, waiting for instructions from King.

Agent Camper stood behind an unmarked government vehicle reciting the plan over to Agent Rodriguez.

"Alright, men we're ready to roll," Agent Camper said.

He grabbed his walkie-talkie and spoke into it.

"Team Bravo, are you in position?"

"Team Bravo, we're here and in position," a voice boomed back.

"Team Alpha, let her rip."

"Roger that," Agent Crown replied.

Agent Crown signaled his men to move on the count of three. "One, two, three!"

An agent smashed a battering ram into the door and immediately backed away. Federal agents filed into the apartment, one behind the other, with guns drawn. They split into three groups and proceeded to raid the place. They found it sparsely furnished for such a large complex. A few tables and couches were spread throughout the apartment, but nothing personal was displayed, like photos or artwork. Then again, this place was supposed to be a hide-out. A sound came from the direction of a closet. Agent Crown opened the door and barged in with his backup in tow. A lone television set was in the center of the room, resting on top of a crate. An agent moved to shut the TV off.

"Don't touch anything!" Agent Crown barked. He was feeling very suspicious.

He glided toward a window that was facing the entrance to the building.

"Nothing's here. It's empty," Agent Crown spoke into the walkie-talkie.

"Nothing there?" someone boomed back.

"Nope. Nothing."

There was dead silence.

King focused his binoculars on the window. He immediately spotted the image he was searching for.

"Go," he said to Ricky.

Ricky was waiting in the car, holding a remote control in his hand. The remote controlled the television inside of the abandoned apartment. He was waiting for King to signal when it was time to flip the switch. Agent Camper heard Agent Crown's response from the walkie-talkie in Agent Cooper's hand.

Empty? he questioned himself. *They called us from this location, less than an hour ago.* He looked at Agent Cooper and said, "Ask Crown if there are any personal belongings inside the apartment."

While he waited for a response from Agent Crown, he got out of the car. Suddenly, it hit him like a bag of bricks. He shouted out to Agent Rodriguez while running toward the building.

"It's a trap! Get them out of there—now!"

Before he could finish shouting his orders, he heard a loud boom followed by a crash.

Glass from the building's windows started to rain down, forcing Agent Camper to duck for cover.

Suddenly, there was a large thud followed by a crash, causing Agent Camper's car to shake. When Agent Camper jumped up, he stared directly into the dead eyes of Agent Crown, who was lying on top of the hood of the car.

66

Agent Camper

For the first time in Agent Camper's career, he found himself entirely speechless. Never in his life had he encountered such an opponent that rendered him helpless. When he was first assigned the case, his arrogance had dictated the usual outcome. He would wait for one of them to fuck up, make an arrest, then make them talk. Now that scenario proved almost impossible. He was starting to blame his director because if he had not proposed this idiotic plan, twelve of his agents would still be alive today. He sat in silence across from the director and watched him enforce another plan that would result in even more destruction.

"You know we can't let her go now," he rambled.

Agent Camper nodded.

He wouldn't say anything. Agent Camper knew the director had finally realized he had fucked up. Director Smith looked for help and was willing to listen, but Agent Camper was not falling for his bullshit. Director Smith was searching for someone to take the fall, and Agent Camper was not willing to be that guy.

"The press is all over this. We let her go now, and we'll look weak and pathetic. What do you think?" he asked Agent Camper.

We? Agent Camper questioned to himself. "You have a point," Agent Camper agreed.

"We need to find a quick solution."

"That's an understatement," Agent Camper replied.

"Alright, here is what I think."

Across town, a dispatcher was calling for a squad unit, to answer a disturbance call in Long Island.

"This is unit nine-zero, responding to a disturbance," answered Officer Kipling.

Officer Kipling and Officer Joyce were two fresh recruits, straight out of the academy. After a year of probation, they were now assigned to street duty as partners. Officer Joyce, a thirty-year-old mother of two, ate in silence in the passenger seat. Officer Kipling, a thirty-four-year-old Caucasian man who was twice divorced was now single and going through a midlife crisis.

"A domestic dispute on the corner of Main Street and Hempstead Avenue, copy," the dispatcher said.

"We copy."

Officer Kipling and Officer Joyce were only three minutes away from where the dispute was reported. They turned on their sirens and zoomed down the block toward the store. As soon as Officer Kipling pulled up in front of the store, Officer Joyce jumped out of the car and proceeded inside. As soon as she entered the store, a man approached her and started rambling on about what he just witnessed.

"I don't know, man. This man and woman walked in together, all hugged up and kissing, then the next minute, they were arguing and shoving each other," Rafael, the grocery store employee, told them.

"Have they frequented the store in the past?" Officer Joyce asked.

"No. I never saw them before. Most of the customers who come here are regulars or live around here. They brought stuff to the counter but never had the chance to pay for anything."

"Then what happened?" Officer Kipling asked, not really caring.

"They started fighting. I asked them to take their fight elsewhere. They left and continued to fight outside, in front of the store. That's when I called you guys."

"Very good. Seems like everything is in order now. We'll file a report, and if they return and start another disturbance, give us a call," Officer Kipling said.

"Thanks a bunch, guys."

"I'll be right out, Joyce, I'm gonna grab a drink. You want anything?" Officer Kipling asked, strutting toward the beverage freezer.

"No thanks. I'll wait for you outside."

Jinx and Bones patiently waited in a double-parked van and watched the cop walk out of the store. Jinx slowly crept behind her as she strolled over to her patrol car. Officer Joyce had her back to the streets and didn't notice Bones standing behind her wearing a mask. He covered her mouth with a chloroform rag, used his right arm to scoop her up by the waist, then threw her into the van. Slamming the door behind him, he relieved the woman of her service revolver and commenced to tie her up. Jinx sped away, giving Geneva and Britney the signal to handle their part of the plan.

Officer Kipling walked toward the car and noticed Officer Joyce was nowhere in sight, so he decided to wait in the car for her. *She's probably somewhere buying food. All she ever thinks about is food,* Kipling thought. He climbed into the car and sat down, not noticing that a motorcycle had jumped the curb.

Geneva steered the bike onto the sidewalk and stopped directly in front of Officer Kipling, who was sitting in the front seat of his patrol car with his legs sticking outside of the car. Britney aimed her .45 colt automatic at the face of the shocked cop. The shots rang out loudly through the night. The soda bottle shattered as the bullets slammed into Officer Kipling's forehead, forcing him to recline onto the driver's seat. Geneva dropped a Haitian flag as she took off, burning rubber while peeling down the block.

67

Pretty Posse

Mrs. Kelly left Meena's house feeling as though she was on top of the world. She headed home to her own apartment. She was so excited that Jerry was back in her life since she did everything he advised her to do on the last night they were together. She left her husband a Dear John letter, packed her bags, and moved out. She found an apartment in Long Island City and quit her job at the school, and now was doing temp work. While she was walking home, she started thinking about everything that went down the past couple of weeks. *Damn, I'm relieved that Jerry is back safely, but sad to know that David is gone. I will definitely miss him.*

She was still in mid-thought as she walked into her building. When she turned the corner to her apartment, she was surprised to find someone waiting in front of her door.

"Hello, Sharon," Jason said, steadying himself to get up off the floor.

"Hel-lo, Ja-son," she replied nervously.

"How have you been? Looking good," Jason said as he stared at Mrs. Kelly from head to toe.

Mrs. Kelly was shocked to see her husband, Lieutenant Jason Kelly, sitting in front of her door waiting for her. *How the fuck did he find me so soon?* she thought.

"What happened, Sharon?" Jason asked.

"Nothing, Jason. You knew where our relationship was headed and it wasn't a secret that I wanted out. I was unhappy."

"But not like this Sharon," Jason slurred.

Damn, he's drunk, she thought, *and it's never a happy ending when he gets like this. He never wants to listen to reason.*

"So, who is he, Sharon? Let's not play games, and don't lie to me because I know there's another man," Jason stated, raising his voice with each word.

Mrs. Kelly didn't respond and slowly moved away from him, wondering if she should run away or deal with the situation.

"I arrived home, only to find a fucking letter saying that you're leaving me! You didn't even give me a chance to say good-bye! What type of shit is that, Sharon? After all that I did for you, you think you can leave me, just like that?" he asked, moving closer to Mrs. Kelly.

"I'm sorry, Jason," she said, her voice quivering.

"Sorry? Sorry? Is that all you can fucking say to me?" he yelled before he lunged at her, grabbing her by the neck and pushing her up against the wall.

"Stop! You're hurting me!" she cried out.

"Imagine how I felt when I got home and found a fucking Dear John letter on the table. My heart was crushed and now you will feel my pain!" Jason hissed, enraged. "You think you can just leave me like that? Well think again, bitch!" Jason said as he tightened his grip around her neck.

Mrs. Kelly's mind was going a hundred miles per minute. *I need to get out of this situation,* she thought as she struggled to loosen his grip. She lifted her right knee up and with all her strength kicked him directly in his balls. Jason instantly released his grip from her neck and dropped to the floor, in agony. Mrs. Kelly gasped, trying to catch her breath, then continued to kick him to ensure he wouldn't be able to get up anytime soon and chase after her. She ran out the building and around the corner, quickly hailing a cab.

Mrs. Kelly arrived at Meena's house thirty minutes later and saw Jerry waiting for her in front of the house. She spoke to him briefly from the cab, but she didn't go into great detail, not wanting the driver to over hear her business. Once the car arrived at the house, she ran out of the car, straight into Jerry's arms.

"What happened, sweetie?" Jerry asked, hugging her.

"That bastard found me! He was waiting in front of my door when I got home, and he put his hands on me, again," she cried.

"He did what?" Jerry asked, examining her face for any visible bruises.

Mrs. Kelly told him exactly what happened and how she was able to escape.

"Don't worry, baby. We're gonna take care of that nigga for you, ASAP. What's his name again, and what precinct does he work for?" Jerry asked.

"His name is Jason Kelly, and he's a lieutenant at the 115th Precinct," Mrs. Kelly responded without hesitation.

Once in the house, Jerry summoned the guys to gather downstairs, and he called a quick meeting to inform them about what had happened to Mrs. Kelly.

"We can add him to the list of pigs we plan on hitting this week," Ricky stated.

"Yo, Jerry," Geneva said, interrupting the brainstorming meeting, "how about you let Pretty Posse handle Mrs. Kelly's situation? I have the perfect setup, and I know how we can make it happen." Geneva wanted to join the fellows in their vendetta. She couldn't stop thinking about the scene at the grocery store. She enjoyed the adrenaline rush she had experienced and wanted that feeling again.

"Okay, Genie, if you think you can handle it then go for it. Just let me know if you need anything from us," Jerry responded with a smile.

"I see someone is hungry," Ricky said, smiling.

"Yeah, hungry and ready to eat," Geneva said, nodding her head.

Geneva walked into the room where Mrs. Kelly was resting and asked her questions about her husband. Geneva informed her Pretty Posse would be handling her situation personally and invited Mrs. Kelly take part if she wanted.

Two days later...

    Lieutenant Jason Kelly was ending his shift for the day and heading out to his favorite after-work spot. It was kind of early, but he didn't want to go home to an empty house. He needed to stay busy because that was the only way he would stop thinking about Sharon. As he was walking out of the precinct, his cell phone began to ring. Jason looked down in his bag to find his phone. With his head still facing down, he turned the corner and walked directly into someone. He was so focused on finding his phone and getting to his destination that he didn't see the person and knocked her cup of coffee right out of her hand. He looked up, about to curse her out for not watching where she was walking until he saw her face and was enchanted by her beauty.

    "Excuse me. I apologize for not paying attention to where I was going. How stupid of me," he said, taking full responsibility and giving her his best smile.

    "Oh no, it's my fault. I should have been paying attention. I have so much on my mind with school and work," the stunning woman said as she shook the coffee off her jacket.

    "How rude of me. My name is Jason. What's yours, if you don't mind my asking?" he said, extending his hand to her when she was done cleaning herself off.

    "I go by Genie," she responded, extending her hand.

    He reached for her right hand and kissed her lightly on her outer palm. "Genie, it was a pleasure bumping into you. May I offer to replace the cup of coffee I spilled all over you?"

    Genie smiled and replied, "I'm not sure. You seem harmless, but you can never tell."

    "Will it make you feel better if I tell you I'm a police officer?" he responded.

    "Maybe, but only if you show me proof that you are in fact an officer," she said, smiling.

    "Okay. Take a look in my bag. There's my uniform and badge. Now, do I pass the test?" he asked, eagerly.

    "Okay, but I get to choose where I want to go," Genie said, hesitantly.

Genie and Jason walked to the end of the corner and got into a cab. Jason was so mesmerized by Genie's exotic beauty he didn't pay attention to where the driver was going. Her smooth tanned complexion, slanted eyes, high cheekbones, and short haircut gave her that seductive look that Jason loved. He asked her all sorts of questions—everything from her age to her occupation and her hobbies.

The cab came to a sudden stop, causing Jason and Genie to jerk forward.

"What's going on?" Jason asked. "Are you okay, Genie?"

"Someone ran out in front of the car, and I had to come to a sudden stop. I hope I didn't hit him," the female cabdriver said.

Jason got out of the car to check and see if anyone had been hit.

"Someone is on the ground!" Jason shouted.

He walked back to the cab and asked the driver, "What is our location?"

"We're on Slate Street," the driver responded.

"I'm going back to check on the injured person. You both stay in the car and call for help," Jason instructed.

Jason walked over to the front of the car to check on the victim who was lying on his stomach with a hood covering his head. He bent to turn the victim over and see if the person had suffered any major injuries and realized it was a woman.

"It's a woman," he said, looking over his shoulder.

Once he turned his head around, Meena flipped on the switch of her stun gun and hit him in the forehead with 400 volts of electricity. His body started convulsing as the surge of currents ran throughout his body. He fell to the ground and began to foam at the mouth while the ladies surrounded him. He looked up and saw three women hovering over him; Geneva, Meena, and Britney. Then, Mrs. Kelly arrived with a bat in hand. She spat on her husband and knocked him out with one swift swing. Ricky and Jerry were two blocks away, waiting for the phone call for them to come and pick up the trash.

"We're ready!" Geneva said.

"We're on our way," Jerry replied.

Ricky and Jerry arrived and found Lieutenant Jason Kelly on the ground unconscious wearing only his underwear. "You ladies are no joke," Ricky said, laughing.

"Pretty Posse at your service," Britney said.

"Now we gag him and throw him in the truck," Ricky said.

"Part two will be in effect tomorrow," Jerry said.

68

Agent Camper

Dozens of pizzas were ordered and delivered throughout various police stations in the borough.

Everyone sat in the office and watched Jenna Hillman report the latest events on television. They were all beyond shock. Nothing more could surprise them when it came to the Body Snatchers.

"Another police officer has been killed tonight, and now two more are missing. Lieutenant Jason Kelly and the other officer who officials believe to be Officer Joyce have been kidnapped. A video tape of the two officers was delivered to our station this morning. The footage is too gruesome to show on TV, but we can tell you that the two victims are still alive. The video shows images of Lieutenant Kelly tied to a chair, gagged, and badly beaten. Officer Joyce was also tied to a chair with a bag over her head. We don't know what the next move of the Body Snatchers will be, but we do know that if they don't get what they want, more lives will be lost. This is Jenna Hillman, signing off."

Agent Camper was way past fatigued and had worn the same clothes for the past two days. He finally gave up brainstorming once he heard about the slaying in Long Island.

The phone rang, but no one moved to answer it.

The secretary walked in saying, "Excuse me, sir. You have an urgent call waiting."

"Who is it?" Director Smith asked, barely audible.

"It's the same caller from before, sir."

Agent Camper jumped to his feet and answered the directors phone.

"Smith," Agent Camper said, lying.

"You have one hour to release Kathy Benton," the voice stated.

"Maybe we can work something out," Agent Camper said, trying a different approach.

"Ahh!" a female voice screamed into the phone. The hairs on the back of Agent Camper's neck stood at attention.

Agent Camper stared at the director who grimaced.

"You have one hour," the voice said, then hung up.

Agent Camper dropped his head in defeat.

"Sir?" Agent Camper.

Director Smith just shook his head.

An hour later...

Sergeant Sterling of the 103rd Precinct in Queens took the pizzas that were delivered to his department and walked back into his office.

Officer Lisbon of the 25th Precinct in Manhattan held the large pizza pies and watched the delivery guy walk away.

Agent Buckingham of 26 Federal Plaza reluctantly accepted the order. He couldn't figure out who ordered all of these pizzas and hadn't informed him in advance. Since he was starving and it wasn't coming out of his pocket, he brought them up to the Antiterrorism Task Force Unit.

Then, the phone rang.

Director Smith was secretly awaiting news regarding the latest disaster.

"Smith," he answered, feeling very tired.

"Look out your window," the caller said.

For some reason, this request frightened the director, and he looked over at Agent Camper with a worried expression. Both the director and Agent Camper walked slowly toward the window. When they looked down, they didn't notice anything out of the ordinary, just cabs and pedestrians rushing to wherever they were heading.

"You see anything?" Director Smith asked.

"No. I do—" Agent Camper said before getting cut off.

Boom!

Not again, he thought.

Director Smith glanced out of the window in amazement. Pedestrians on the ground started running frantically. Fireballs, shards of glass, and ashes flew out of spaces where windows once were.

A federal building!

The phone rang again.

"Smith."

"Are you watching the news?" the caller asked.

"And this is?" Detective Smith asked in frustration.

"Governor Long."

"Yeah, we know. A federal building has just been bombed," Detective Smith said, dropping into his seat.

"What? A federal building?" the governor shouted.

"I thought that was why you called," Detective Smith said.

"No! I was calling to tell you that the 25th, and 103rd Precincts have been bombed. Now what is this about a federal building?"

Agent Camper shook his head. *That's it. I quit,* he thought.

"We'll have to call you back, governor. I have an urgent matter to attend to," Detective Smith said, hanging up. He sighed. "Get the district attorney!"

On the other side of town, Frank Lucci sat back in amusement as he watched the news.

"I can't fucking believe this!" he said as he lit a cigar and began to laugh. "You hear that? Now that's news!" he yelled, slapping Lucky on his shoulders.

Lucky wore a neutral expression. He did not want Frankie to know how he really felt. Lucky enjoyed the justice system getting a taste of their own medicine. He just didn't like who was behind it, so he kept his mouth shut.

"Get me a fucking bottle. This calls for a celebration!" Frankie ordered. *The kid did it.*

EPILOGUE

Everyone huddled in front of the TV. Jerry was very pleased with the way everyone stuck with him through the rough times, especially Ricky, Jinx, and Bones because without them, things would have proved to be very difficult—even impossible. He was more surprised by the fact that the women held themselves down like true soldiers. With all the trouble and turmoil he went through, he knew he was fortunate to have such a loyal crew. Now, if everything went as planned, the only thing he would have to worry about was what to do about his relationship with Mrs. Kelly and Fifi.

"Everyone, hush down! The news is back on!" Geneva shouted.

Meena sat on Gully's lap, and Bones and Jinx sat beside Ricky who was finessing a blunt. Jerry was holding Barbara while Loria sat between Lauren, Mrs. Kelly, and Fifi. Everyone appeared anxious and seemed to be sitting at the edge of their seats.

"Now, with the latest on the Body Snatchers fiasco, District Attorney Gregory Hardaway will speak about the case involving Katherine Benton, the mother of alleged Body Snatcher, Jerry Benton. Will they release her, or will they keep her in custody?" Jenna asked.

"Radicals have been protesting for the release of Ms. Benton. Protesters feel the arrest was senseless and will only lead to more bloodshed. Now, live on the scene, is Jack Sway."

Jerry leaned forward.

"The officers of the United States Attorney General would like to send our condolences to the families and friends of the officers and agents that were killed in the line of duty," he stated. "We have yet to receive information on the investigation of the Body Snatchers. Our confidential informants are being thoroughly interrogated and are willing to cooperate with our agencies. At the moment, we are investigating substantial leads regarding the Body Snatchers' whereabouts, but due to the lack of evidence, the federal judge has now ordered the release of Katherine Benton."

"In other news, Officer Joyce, who was also kidnapped by the Body Snatchers was found bound and gagged, but alive. She was found in Rockaway Beach Queens. There is still no word on the whereabouts of Lieutenant Jason Kelly.

The room burst with applause and screams of joy.

"That's what the fuck I'm talking about!" Bones said, giving dap to Jinx.

"I'm so happy for you!" Mrs. Kelly jumped up and hugged Jerry.

"Yo, light that shit up!" Britney said.

Jerry looked up to the ceiling and said a short prayer of thanks. *This is for you, David,* thought a tearful Jerry.

"Hold up, my man. Before y'all light that shit up, tell 'em what we are," Jerry said, standing.

Everyone smiled and said, "Haitians4Life!"

Love on the Rocks

School was out, and I was excited I passed the sixth grade. It was looking kind of shaky at first, but I did it. Running into the building, I knew the elevator was out of order, so I ran up the six flights of stairs leading to my apartment. The elevators rarely worked in this place. If we were lucky, we would get a week of service during a month. You see, I was born in Brooklyn in Brookdale Hospital and was raised in the infamous Red Hook projects. I got used to a certain way of life in my neighborhood. With my report card in hand and wearing a big cheesy smile spread across my face, I ran through my apartment, shouting out at the top of my lungs for my momma. I couldn't have felt any happier at that moment.

We lived in the first building once you entered the projects. Our building only had six floors, and we lived on the fifth. Our two-bedroom apartment was facing the front of the building. It included a kitchen, bathroom, and living room. There was nothing glamorous about the place. A few family memorabilia were sprawled throughout the house. Cheap souvenirs and electronics equipment were placed somewhat strategically within the living room in order to make up for the emptiness in the apartment. We had dusty furniture that had been in the family for over a decade, and it was still covered in plastic. No *MTV Cribs* for this apartment.

This year had taken a toll on all of us. My grades started to slip in the middle of the school year because I missed so many classes. I had to pick up some of the slack around the house and find ways to come up with money in order to help Momma with the bills. A lot of my absences were due to me working odd jobs around the neighborhood. My teachers threatened I would have to repeat the sixth grade if I continued missing school. I stepped it up, studied hard, and did extra credit work.. It all paid off in the end because I received a passing grade and was now going into the seventh grade. I still continued to do odd jobs on the weekends in order to earn money.

With my book bag slung over my shoulder, I barged into the kitchen and found Momma sitting at the kitchen table looking out the window.

"Momma, I passed! I did it, Ma!" I exclaimed, waving the card in the air in excitement.

My momma always seemed worried and appeared frail and thin, and was starting to age quickly. Her striking eyes were filled with wisdom and pain. Her complexion was no longer smooth, dark and radiant. Now it seemed dull and ashen. She was dressed in her favorite burgundy bathrobe as she blew a cloud of cigarette smoke out of the window. Still maintaining my smile, I approached her saying, "Did you hear me, Momma? I'm going into the seventh grade."

As if noticing me for the first time, Momma just stared at me. Ignoring my instincts, I continued,

"Look, Momma, everybody thought I was gonna fail, and I didn't. I showed them, Momma!" I said, filled with excitement..

While blowing smoke in my direction she replied in a low, raspy voice, "Why da hell you yelling at me like you ain't got no damn sense?"

My smile slowly faded.

"Why you so damn happy, huh? What the hell got you smiling in my face like you crazy or something?" she slurred.

She's drunk again, I thought. Ever since Pop died, Momma was slowly taking her own life away. It had been hard for me to see her like this. Lately, that liquor bottle had become a permanent fixture in her world. While staring down at the ground, I slowly said, "Nothing, Momma. I just wanted to let you know I made it into junior high and wanted to show you my report card."

"Does it come with money?" she barked.

"No, ma'am," I mumbled.

In a sudden outburst, she banged her fist on the table and demanded I look at her when she spoke to me.

Willing myself not to cry, I slowly raised my head and met her eyes.

I said, "Does it come with some damn money?" she growled.

"No, ma'am," I replied sullenly.

"Then, what the hell am I suppose to do with yo' damn grades when the bill collector comes knocking for his money, huh?" she shouted, nearly falling off her seat.

Shifting from leg to leg, I didn't respond.

"You think I can show yo' damn grades when he wants his money?" she slurred.

With each passing second, she seemed to become more and more like a stranger to me.

"We need some money, Eric!" she shouted. "It's money that moves this world, not grades," she said, then paused. "What you gonna do now?"

"I'm gonna find some money," I replied mechanically.

"Good," she said and sat back down .

"Don't come back until you get some," she warned, lighting her cigarette and taking another swig from her whiskey bottle.

I always tried avoiding her when she got like this, only sometimes I couldn't. It is times like this that I wish I never knew her and wished she wasn't my mother. Clearly defeated, I did exactly as I was told. I dropped my report card on the floor, walked out of the kitchen, and out of the apartment, never to return home again.

"Where did you go?" Dr. Taylor asked me while taking notes.

I was in one of my sessions with Dr. Taylor when I told him about the last time I spoke to my mother. Dr. Taylor was a middle-aged psychiatrist whom I had chosen when I recently decided to seek therapy. I had been thinking about my past a lot lately, and I thought he might be able to help me understand why.

Dr. Taylor's office was located in Manhattan near Chambers Street a couple of train stops from where I worked. His office was on the eighteenth floor, and it occupied the entire space. The atmosphere of the office was very mellow, making you feel at ease as soon as you walked through the door. Once you entered, the receptionist was there to greet you. The walls were an earth-tone color, and the dim lighting and soft jazz music playing in the background created a relaxing atmosphere. The walls were decorated with certificates and degrees displaying Dr. Taylor's accomplishments in psychology. African artifacts were placed on top of some of his furniture, showing his Ethiopian heritage. With the windows shut, the room was almost quiet enough to hear each other breathe. I was lying on the therapist's couch as I strolled down memory lane and finished my story about my last days living with Momma.

"I ran out the door and around the corner for a li'l bit, then went to my cousin Lamont's house," I said, staring up at the ceiling.

"Why did you decide not to return home?" I heard him ask.

I sighed, just thinking about how I felt that day.

"I don't know. I guess I was just tired of it all. Sometimes I would go home and find her sprawled out on the living room floor, sleeping in her vomit. I'd clean her up and take her to her bedroom. There were nights when she would curse me out because I wasn't able to bring home any money. But that was my momma. We weren't dirt poor or anything, but we had just enough to get by. Even my odds jobs that paid me off the books didn't make Momma happy. It was never enough for her. There wasn't enough to pay the bills because she spent it buying bottles of whiskey that she couldn't live without. I knew this and I sacrificed my childhood for her. I missed out on all the fun times my friends were having because the little money I had went to supporting her habit. She had no idea what I went through or how tough it was because of her. Growing up in the projects wasn't easy, man," I said, feeling anger build up inside me.

Silence filled the room.

I never liked talking about those days. Only Lamont knew how crazy and hard those days were on me. I had to move in with my aunt Shelly because of Momma. I was thankful for Aunt Shelly because if it wasn't for her, I know I wouldn't be here right now, struggling to tell my stories to Dr. Taylor, I thought.

Coming Soon

Butter by Marlon Green

A Liar & A Cheat by Monette

At Your Best by Raymond Francis

Body Snatchers II by Rozè